The last of her resistance slipped away. "You win," she whispered.

"I win? You think this a game to me?"

"If it is, you don't play to lose."

"I'm just mad attracted to you," he said. "Am I the only one feeling this?"

Maybe it was the vulnerable hitch to his voice, the rawness of emotion she heard. Maybe it was the earnest look in his eyes. The look that said he was unable to control whatever it was that seemed to have him in its grip. She understood. Because she felt the same way, too.

Lorraine repositioned herself on the sofa so that her legs were beneath her and her body was facing Hunter's. "I feel it, too," she admitted. He had put himself out on an emotional ledge, and she didn't want to leave him there alone. To make him believe that she wasn't as interested in him as he was in her would have been dishonest and cruel. God only knew why she was attracted to him, but she was. Fiercely.

Dear Reader,

Welcome back to Ocean City and Fire Station Two, the backdrop for my Love on Fire series. This time, you'll join Lorraine and Hunter on their journey to find love.

Have you ever let a disagreement come between you and a family member? What if that estranged family member died? That's what my hero, Hunter, faces. He's a strong and driven firefighter, but the death of his father brings him to his knees. It's certainly not an ideal time to meet the irresistible Lorraine, but his connection with her is as undeniable as it is welcome. Until Hunter learns something about her that he's not sure he can get past.

It's with some sadness that I say goodbye to Ocean City and the sexy firefighters I've written about. But I'm excited about my new series featuring the Burke brothers. These four single, athletic brothers are going to sweep you off of your feet! Get ready for some steamy stories!

Thanks so much for picking up *Sizzling Desire*. I hope you enjoy Hunter and Lorraine's story!

Kayla

Sizzling
DESIRE

Kayla Perrin

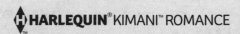
HARLEQUIN® KIMANI™ ROMANCE

Recycling programs
for this product may
not exist in your area.

ISBN-13: 978-0-373-86520-8

Sizzling Desire

Printed in U.S.A.

Kayla Perrin is a multi-award winning, multi-published *USA TODAY* and *Essence* bestselling author. She's been writing since she could hold a pencil, and sent her first book to a publisher when she was just thirteen years old. Since 1998, she's had over fifty novels and novellas published. She's been featured in *Ebony* magazine, *RT Book Reviews*, the *South Florida Business Journal*, the *Toronto Star* and other Canadian and American publications. Her works have been translated into Italian, German, Spanish and Portuguese. In 2011, Kayla received the prestigious Harry Jerome Award for excellence in the arts in Canada. She lives in the Toronto area with her daughter.

You can find Kayla on Facebook, Twitter and Instagram. Please visit her website at authorkaylaperrin.com.

Books by Kayla Perrin

Harlequin Kimani Romance

Visit the Author Profile page at Harlequin.com for more titles.

In memory of Byron Askie Nedd.

By all accounts, you were one of the nicest guys ever.

I miss your warm spirit, your kind heart and your music.

As they say, the good ones die young.

RIP, my friend.

Chapter 1

The pulsing beat of the music in the bar thrummed through Lorraine Baxter's body. As she looked at her three best friends in the world, who were all seated around her at the table, she halted her head-bopping as a wave of emotion washed over her. "I love you guys so much," she said, her eyes misting as she looked at each of them in turn. "You know that, right? Every time I need you, you guys are there for me. You *never* fail me. So thank you for always being there. And thanks so much for being here for me tonight."

"Where else would we be?" Rosa asked, giving Lorraine's hand a squeeze. She was five foot nothing, part Mexican and part African American. She had a mass of long, curly black hair that flowed down her back and around her shoulders, hair that she hadn't cut in about a decade. Whenever she went out, she liked to show off her voluptuous figure. Tonight she was doing that by wearing a low cut, formfitting black dress that highlighted her "girls"—as she liked to call them.

"Of course we're here for you," Amanda said. "This is the most important day of your life."

Amanda was tall, five foot nine, with a slender frame and smooth, dark skin. She liked to wear her hair short and away from her face. She had beautiful eyes and perfect cheekbones, features that were highlighted when she wore her black hair back.

"It is, isn't it?" Lorraine asked, the significance of today once again dawning on her. She was a newly single woman, her divorce final now for six and a half hours. She raised her glass, which was filled with an icy margarita brew. "To dear friends. The ones a girl can really count on through the good and the bad in life."

Rosa, Amanda and Trina all raised their glasses with their own drinks and held them high. "Hear, hear," and "Cheers!" they said in unison, before sipping their respective drinks.

Lorraine had met these three women in college. They'd all been in the same sociology class, and tended to sit in the same seats, which coincidentally were near each other. One day, Rosa had been crying softly throughout the lecture, and Trina had ended up talking to her. Lorraine, who'd overheard bits of the conversation that had to do with some guy who'd dumped her, had inserted herself into the conversation to offer Rosa comfort. Amanda had done the same. It had been Amanda's idea that they all go out to have a drink and talk about the class assignment as a way to help Rosa's mood. Ever since that day, they'd all been friends.

"I think we need a round of tequila shooters," Trina announced, already pushing her chair back. Trina was also tall, just about an inch shorter than Amanda. Her skin was very pale, and on occasion people confused her for Hispanic. But she would proudly point out that her thick hips, big booty and kinky brown hair were sure signs that she was African American.

"You *always* think we need tequila," Amanda said to Trina, then laughed.

"Because life is better with tequila."

"Not my life," Rosa quipped.

Trina looked down at her, giving her a pointed stare. "If not for the round of tequila shooters that day after sociology class when we first met, would we even be friends right now?"

Lorraine remembered that day well. Trina had assured Rosa that tequila would help her forget whatever guy was causing her so much emotional grief. Rosa had downed the tequila shot and promptly gagged. They'd all laughed about it, but through the laughter, Rosa realized she was no longer thinking about the guy who'd broken her heart. So tequila shooters were always on the menu whenever there was some sort of man drama among the group.

"All right," Rosa agreed. "But one tequila shooter is my limit."

"Oh, we already know that!" Amanda said as Trina started off toward the bar. "Ah, this is just like old times. A round of shooters will kick this celebration into high gear." She faced Lorraine. "And you—no more tears!"

Lorraine nodded. Tonight *was* a celebration. That had been the plan, to go out with her friends. She certainly hadn't wanted to mark the occasion at home alone.

"Okay," Lorraine agreed. "No more tears. Not that I'm crying over Paul," she added with a frown.

"Good!" Rosa exclaimed. "You're rid of that jerk who made your life a living hell. You should be dancing on the table!"

Lorraine couldn't help smiling. "That would go over well with this crowd, me jumping on the table and getting down."

"I'll give you one hundred dollars to get on the table and do it," Amanda said. "If I were finally free of such a nasty jerk, I'd be dancing on the roof."

"Ah, no." Lorraine wasn't about to make a spectacle of herself. Though she certainly did want to dance for joy. She was finally free of Paul. A marriage that never should have happened.

Rather, a marriage that she had entered into whole-heartedly, only to learn that her husband hadn't given their union the same effort. Paul had never truly loved her, never supported her dreams and goals. Ending the marriage was the only thing to do.

Lorraine had expected him to be unhappy, but not for him to turn downright nasty during the divorce proceedings. He'd had an investigator look into her financial history, find out if she had secret bank accounts, or gifts from family she'd never told Paul about. The slimy investigator had learned that her mother had left her a bond. Nothing substantial, but Paul had nonetheless demanded half of it.

Thinking about Paul left a bitter taste in her mouth, and Lorraine sipped some water. Her divorce was final. Paul was officially out of her life. And tonight, she was wiping the slate clean fittingly. Taking back her single status with grand style. Rosa had even bought her a black veil— the opposite of the white one she'd worn on her wedding day. Not to mark this is as a somber occasion, but to mark it as a funeral for her past life. A life she could officially move on from.

"I'm sure this is an emotional day for you," Rosa said. "Saying goodbye to the past can be hard, even if you know it's the right thing." She smiled softly. "I look forward to the day when you're back to being your old self—the woman who was stress-free and happy until Paul dragged you down."

Rosa was absolutely right. Lorraine hadn't been the same person after just two years of marriage. She'd sunk into depression. Nothing had been good enough to please Paul. All her efforts to make her marriage work had been in vain. She had increasingly thrown herself into work, but even that was an emotional rollercoaster. As a palliative care nurse, she loved her patients, but losing them was always painful.

"Trina needs to hurry up with those shooters," Amanda said.

Lorraine looked toward the section of the bar where

Trina had ventured off to. Trina was lost somewhere in the crowd.

As Lorraine's gaze wandered the other way, it stopped abruptly, landing on another pair of eyes. They were dark and intense and drew her in for a few glorious seconds. She stared, unable to turn away, while the man who owned those striking eyes stared back.

The air rushing out of her lungs, Lorraine felt an undeniable sizzle of heat.

She checked out the man staring back at her. Golden brown skin. Broad shoulders and seriously muscular biceps. *Wow.*

She glanced away, blushing.

"Who are you looking at?" Amanda asked, and shot a peek over her shoulder.

"Don't!" Lorraine admonished, but she was too late.

"What am I missing?" Rosa asked.

"Oh, I see him," Amanda said, her tone piquing with interest. "The guy behind me in the second booth. Wearing a pale blue shirt."

"*Oh!*" Rosa's eyes widening, she playfully swatted Lorraine's arm. "Girl, you're *flirting*?"

"Can't I look at a man without you guys making a big deal about it?" Lorraine asked.

Trina appeared then, weaving through the crowd back toward the table. She was carrying a plate with the four shot glasses grouped closely together. Surrounding the glasses were four lime wedges. "One round of tequila shooters!" Trina announced. She placed the plate onto the table, then took her seat beside Amanda again. "Grab one, ladies."

They each took a shot glass, but left the limes on the plate. Trina was the first to lick her hand and pour salt onto it. The rest of the ladies followed suit.

Rosa quickly raised her shot glass. "To Lorraine getting to know the hot guy in the blue shirt."

Trina frowned. "Huh? What did I miss?"

"He's at the table behind us," Amanda explained.

"Don't look—" Lorraine said, but Trina was already whipping her head around.

Lorraine glanced at the hottie again, saw him smile at her. Oh, God. He was paying attention to them. And now he knew that she and her friends were talking about him.

"I'm totally embarrassed," Lorraine said. "He knows that I'm staring at him. Thanks to you guys."

"To Lorraine's fresh start," Amanda said, raising the shooter and wiggling her eyebrows suggestively.

"I'll drink to that!" Rosa enthused.

There was no point in arguing with these women, who loved her unconditionally. So Lorraine downed her shooter along with her friends. The tequila burned its way down her throat. She quickly stuffed the lime in her mouth to kill the bite of the booze. As she and her friends did the same, Rosa feigned a gagging sound. They all started laughing. Yeah, this was just like old times.

"Okay, that's my one and only tequila shot for the night," Rosa said. "No more."

"As if we don't know that," Trina said. "Though I'm really curious to know what a two-tequila night would be like for you."

"You're not going to find out," Rosa told her.

As her friends engaged in playful chatter, Lorraine glanced in the sexy stranger's direction. Again, he was looking at her.

"If you're going to keep flirting," Rosa began, "you need to fix your makeup. It's a mess from when you got teary a few minutes ago."

"What?" Lorraine gasped, horrified.

Rosa got to her feet and reached for Lorraine's hand. "Let's go to the restroom."

Lorraine didn't protest. Not that she was interested in the man she'd noticed, but flirting was *not* sexy with raccoon eyes.

She grabbed her purse from the table and started for the restroom with Rosa, who was a little unsteady on her feet. Lorraine's head was definitely lighter. The margarita was already having an effect on her. She wasn't about to get over-the-top drunk, but being tipsy and feeling good was exactly what she wanted. Especially since she hadn't hung out with her friends like this in such a long time. Paul hadn't expressly forbidden it, but he'd made it clear that he didn't like her friends. So they all needed tonight, and there was no shame in letting loose. They were all taking taxis home, so no need to worry about any of them driving while drunk.

Lorraine and Rosa entered the bathroom. The dark red walls seemed to suck up the already dim light. It was a horrible color scheme for the visibility required to reapply makeup.

Lorraine headed toward a mirror while Rosa went into a stall. Dim lighting or not, her ruined makeup was clear to see. Her mascara and eyeliner had bled around her eyes, and there was one long black streak on the left side of her face. She wondered if the hottie had been able to see her face clearly. How embarrassing!

Two other women burst into the restroom, giggling. As Lorraine tore off a piece of paper towel, the young women went right for the mirror, fixing their hair and applying fresh coats of lipstick.

"You really think he's into me?" one of the women asked. She couldn't have been more than twenty-two.

"He wouldn't have bought you a drink if he wasn't," her friend responded.

Lorraine wet the paper towel, then started to carefully wipe around her eyes to remove the mess. She smiled as she listened to the friends chatter about the guy one of them liked. How long had it been since she'd been out like this with her own friends, happily scoping out the available men? Not in forever.

She frowned. What if the sexy stranger had been checking her out because of her black veil? She'd noticed curious looks from others tonight, but something about this man intrigued her. She hoped there was a connection between them.

The black streaks cleaned, Lorraine reached into her purse for her compact and started applying a fresh coat of powder.

Rosa exited the stall and approached a sink. When she looked at Lorraine she said, "*Much* better."

"You mean the raccoon look isn't my thing?" Lorraine joked.

"On Halloween, yes. But tonight, not so much."

Lorraine laughed. Then, once again looking at her reflection, she asked, "Should I change my lipstick?"

"You actually have something other than the boring brown you're wearing? That *is* the name of the lipstick, isn't it? Boring Brown."

Lorraine cut her eyes at her friend. She liked the brown color. It went with everything. And it was a good choice for her caramel-colored complexion. But as she stared at herself in the mirror, she had to admit that the color didn't add any pizzazz. Compared to the two women at the other end of the mirror, wearing bright colors on their lips and their eyes, Lorraine's look was...well, boring indeed.

Lorraine dug her other lipstick choice out of her purse. While Rosa went to dry her hands, Lorraine applied a coat of the red and pressed her lips together.

Her eyes widened. After her initial shock, her lips

spread in a slow smile. What a dramatic difference. Her lips looked extra kissable.

Extra kissable… Good grief. Maybe it was the alcohol getting to her.

"Great veil."

Lorraine turned to look at the two young women, who were staring at her in awe. "Oh, thanks."

"Single and ready to mingle!" one of them said. "You go, girl." Then, linking arms, they both headed out of the bathroom.

Lorraine smiled, then looked at her reflection again. The veil *was* great. Perhaps a little over the top, but she'd worn a veil when getting married. Why not now when she was out celebrating her divorce?

"What's the name of that color?" Rosa asked.

Lorraine turned the lipstick container over and looked at the bottom. "One Night Stand," she read. "Good Lord."

Rosa beamed at her. "Perfect."

"Perfect?" Lorraine's eyes widened. "Girl, you're crazy."

"Hey, you never know. You already have a prospect…"

But Lorraine did know. Unlike the women who'd just left the restroom, she wasn't looking for a hookup. She didn't want anything tonight except a little harmless flirting, and a lot of fun with her friends. Tomorrow she would sleep in and recover from her late night out, because at thirty-two there was no way she could recover as quickly as she had when she'd partied at twenty.

Lorraine fixed the veil around her face and nodded at her reflection, satisfied.

"Gorgeous," Rosa told her.

"Thanks." Lorraine put her makeup back in her purse. "I still have to use the toilet. You don't have to wait for me."

"You sure?"

"Yeah. I'll be fine. I'll be out soon."

Lorraine took a few more minutes in the bathroom. Right before she headed out, she decided to spritz herself with a little perfume. Just in case she and the sexy stranger spoke or danced.

Lorraine was securing the latch on her purse so her head was down as she exited the restroom. As she lifted her gaze, she saw a man ease his body off the wall and start in her direction, almost as if he'd been waiting for her. As he neared her, he grinned. Good God, was this stranger she'd never seen before actually approaching her?

"Excuse me," Lorraine said, and sidestepped him when he put himself directly in her path.

"Not so fast," the man said. He took her by the arm, forcing her to stop, then stepped in front of her. "Now that you have me alone, you don't have anything to say to me? You playing shy?"

Lorraine looked at up at him, flummoxed. "Excuse me?"

"I saw you making eyes at me out there."

Lorraine was confused. And then it hit her. This guy must have been somewhere close to the sexy stranger. He thought she'd been hitting on *him*.

"I'm sorry," she said. "You're mistaken."

She made another move to step past him, but he surprised her by slipping an arm around her waist and pulling her against his thick body. "Come on, you don't have to be bashful."

"No, seriously." She tried to extricate herself from his grasp. "I wasn't flirting with you. Sorry if you got that impression." She didn't want to offend him, just in case he was irrational. She could tell by the slight slurring of his voice that he'd been drinking too much. Men who drank too much could be a problem.

"You're beautiful," he whispered into her ear.

He held her tighter as she continued to try to free herself, and that's when she truly became alarmed. "Let me go." She spoke in a firm voice. "I don't want this."

"I just want to get to know you," the man said.

"This isn't okay," Lorraine said.

"Let the lady go."

At the sound of the commanding voice, the man loosened his grip on Lorraine but didn't fully release her. He looked beyond Lorraine to the man who'd spoken.

"What, is this your girl?"

Finally, Lorraine was able to pull herself free. She did and turned. And felt as though she'd been kicked in the stomach.

The man coming to her defense was none other than the man she'd been flirting with!

"When a woman tells you to let her go," her sexy savior said, "you let her go."

There was such air of authority about him that he was even hotter to her now than he had been before. Was he a cop?

The man who'd been harassing Lorraine stepped away, raising his hands in a sign of surrender. He probably feared he was going to get his lights knocked out by this man, who was taller and clearly stronger than he — if all those perfectly honed muscles were any indication. "Sorry, dude."

The man walked toward them briskly. "Don't apologize to me. Apologize to her."

The harasser looked at Lorraine with a sheepish expression. "Sorry about that. I just thought… You know."

"It's fine," Lorraine said tersely. It wasn't actually fine. She hated men who got drunk and felt it was their right to become aggressive with women.

Fortunately, the jerk promptly took off, leaving Lorraine alone with the stranger.

"Are you okay?" he asked her. His deep voice sent delicious shivers down her spine.

Lorraine looked up at Mr. Too Fine. He had to be around six foot three. Golden brown skin, dark eyes framed by thick, curly lashes. "Yes," she said, nodding. "I'm fine."

"He didn't hurt you?"

"I think you came just in time. I was starting to get worried."

"I'm glad I got here when I did, then."

"Yeah. Me, too." Lorraine's pulse was pounding. She glanced away, nervous.

"What's with the veil?" the guy asked. Then, "Oh, wait. It's black, not white. So the opposite of a wedding... Right?"

"Wedding?" Lorraine scoffed with a smile. "What wedding? I'm no longer married." *Single and ready to mingle!*

"I get it." The man smiled down at her, and he had the cutest dimples.

"I'm Hunter," he said, extending his hand.

Lorraine accepted it. His warm grip enveloped hers and sent a zap of heat coursing through her veins. "I'm... I'm Mary."

Why was she lying?

"Nice to meet you, Mary," he said. "What are you drinking?"

"Margaritas," she answered without hesitation. Then she felt a little silly. Did she really want him to buy her a drink or two? Any more to drink and she might not be able to think too clearly.

Single and ready to mingle! The parting words of the young woman leaving the restroom jumped into her mind again. Lorraine couldn't help it—she started giggling.

Hunter narrowed his eyes as he looked at her, though the edges of his lips were curved in a grin. "What's so funny?"

What indeed? What was it about this man that had her acting like a school girl?

"I don't even know," Lorraine said. "I really have no clue why I'm laughing."

Hunter's grin widened. He seemed to like what she'd said. "High on life, I guess?" he suggested.

"Something like that."

"You ready to go back out there?" he asked, offering her his elbow.

Lorraine looped her hand through his arm, feeling a flash of heat as her skin once again connected with his. His arm was strong. He had rock-hard muscles. This guy was seriously hot.

"Sure," she said.

"Then let's go get that drink."

Chapter 2

Lorraine saw her friends' stunned looks as she came out from the restroom area holding on to the arm of a tall, dark and sexy brother. Smiling with smug satisfaction, Lorraine gave them all a little wave as she walked with Hunter past their table to the bar.

"You know why I'm here tonight," Lorraine said to Hunter as they neared the bar. "What brings you here?"

"I'm new in town," Hunter explained.

"Ahhh. Are you new to California?" Lorraine asked. "Did you move here from another state?"

"I did, yes. But I'm not new to Ocean City. I grew up here, then moved to Reno when I hit eighteen. I lived and worked there for sixteen years, and now I'm back. I'm a firefighter."

That explained why he was in such good shape. Firefighters were strong, their bodies immaculately honed in order to be able to rescue people from burning buildings and other disastrous situations. No wonder he had come to her aid in such a chivalrous way.

She swayed a little—deliberately—so she could wrap her fingers tighter around his arm. Yes, she was shamelessly copping a feel. She barely even recognized herself.

"Oops," Hunter said, securing his hand on her back to make sure she was steady. "You okay?"

"I'm fine," Lorraine said. "You're so sweet." *And so hot.*

So hot that she wanted to smooth her hands over his muscular pecs for a few glorious minutes.

She turned away from him and continued toward the bar. What was going on with her? It must be the alcohol making her react so strongly to this man.

Though the truth was, she didn't care *what* was bringing out this reaction in her. Because every time Hunter looked at her, she felt incredibly desirable—something she hadn't felt with Paul since the early days of their marriage. But unlike her ex-husband, Hunter's attraction for her was obvious in that dark, intense gaze. Every time their eyes connected, the chemistry sizzled.

Lorraine's heart was pounding with excitement, and it was a wonderful feeling after all the pain and heartache she'd gone through recently. It was nice to feel the pitter-patter of her pulse because of a guy who rated eleven out of ten on the sexy scale.

Lorraine veered to the left to sidestep a group of women. And all of a sudden, her heel twisted beneath her body. This time, she started to go down in earnest. Hunter quickly swooped his arms around her, and the next thing she knew, he was scooping her into his arms.

"Oh, my God," she uttered. "You're not carrying me—"

"Can't have you breaking an ankle."

He was actually carrying her to the bar. All eyes in the vicinity looked at them, some people chuckling, some gaping. Lorraine should have been embarrassed, but instead she tightened her arms around Hunter's neck and held on, smiling from ear to ear. When was the last time anyone had carried her like this? She may as well enjoy the ride.

Once at the bar, Hunter lowered Lorraine onto a stool. "There you go," he said.

She looked up at him coyly, biting down on the bottom of her ruby-red lip.

He grinned at her, his gaze lingering on hers. Then he leaned across the bar to order drinks. Lorraine shamelessly checked out his form. With his hands resting on the bar, the muscles on the backs of his arms grew taut. His wide back tapered to a slim waist. His behind even looked muscular in the black dress pants. He had the kind of body that running backs in those tight football outfits had. The kind of physique she had been appreciating daily for the past several months in the current Ocean City firefighters calendar. Though in her opinion, he was hotter—and there were a *lot* of fine men in that calendar.

A couple of minutes later, he turned toward her holding a margarita. Lorraine carefully took the glass from him. For himself, Hunter had a bottle of beer. He clinked the top of his bottle gently against her glass, then they both took a sip.

"I probably should get back to my friends," Lorraine said after a minute.

"Or—we could get out of here."

"Pardon me?" Lorraine asked.

"Nothing," Hunter said.

She narrowed her eyes. Was she hearing things? Or had he just suggested that they leave the bar together?

"I'll walk you back to your table," Hunter told her, and extended his arm to her again.

She took a liberal sip of her drink before accepting Hunter's arm. He helped her down from the stool. She continued to hold on to him as she walked. He led her to her table, where her friends were all looking at her with wide-eyed gazes.

Trina was the first to speak. "Someone's made a new friend." She shot Lorraine a devious smile. "I'm Trina." She extended her hand. "And you are?"

"Hunter," he said, shaking her hand.

"And that's Rosa and Amanda," Lorraine said, pointing to each of her friends in turn. She felt a moment of panic. They could blow her cover. If one of them blurted out her real name…

It was silly, but she'd lied to Hunter about her name and didn't want him to find out the truth. She placed a hand on the back of his arm and said, "You know what? Why don't we hit the dance floor?"

"Oh." Hunter sounded surprised. "Sure."

Lorraine started to sway her body to the music. Then she took him by the hand and led him to the back of the bar, where the dance floor was. She started to shake her hips to the pulsing R&B beat before they were even on the floor. Finding an available spot near one corner, Lorraine turned to face Hunter. She kicked up the movements of her body, her hips and legs moving in tune with the rhythm.

Hunter watched her for several seconds, then leaned close and slipped his arm around her waist. "You're gorgeous, you know that?"

"Is this how you flatter all the women you rescue?" Lorraine asked.

"What other women?" Hunter countered. "There's one woman in the bar I can't take my eyes off of. And that's you, Mary."

She looped her arms around his neck, and although the tempo of the music was fast, they both started moving more slowly. They were moving to their own beat, as if oblivious to the world around them.

"You know what I don't understand?" Hunter asked.

"What?"

"How some guy would let you go. If you were mine, I'd never let you out of my sight."

"Is that so?"

Hunter pulled his bottom lip between his teeth as he stared into her eyes. "Definitely."

Good Lord, he was arousing her with his seductive looks and his words. Her feminine core began to throb.

"I *really* want to kiss you," he whispered into her ear.

Tingles of delight spread through Lorraine's body. Her breathing deepened. "Really?"

"Really." His voice was husky, filled with desire. He was the sexiest man she'd ever been this close to.

"Then why don't you?" Lorraine whispered on a shuddery breath. She trailed her fingers along his nape, and when he made a soft groaning sound, she felt a surge of feminine power. He reached up and gently stroked her cheek, then caught her chin between his thumb and forefinger and angled her face up to his. Every nerve in Lorraine's body went taut with expectation as Hunter lowered his head down to hers.

Lorraine parted her lips. And then his mouth pressed against hers, slow, sweet, succulent. It was the kind of kiss that promised something more.

Hot, sweating bodies between the sheets.

A night of carnal bliss.

Beneath her veil, he tangled his fingers in her hair, holding her in place. His lips moved faster over hers, his teeth gently nipping, his tongue flicking out and running along her bottom lip. Lorraine gasped from the onslaught of sensations.

"Oh, yes," Hunter moaned, and then flicked his tongue over hers.

She couldn't remember a kiss setting her body on fire like this. And then she giggled. Who was the best person to put out a fire but a fireman? Good grief. What was with these corny thoughts in her head?

"Are you laughing?" Hunter whispered against her cheek. "You don't like this?"

"I love it," Lorraine told him. She continued to run her fingers along the base of his neck, reveling in the way his breaths deepened. Then she pressed her body against his, feeling the evidence of his desire for her. Hard, thick. Impressive. "You're making me forget we're in a crowded bar."

Hunter's lips curved into a grin. He looked down at her, and she up at him. And she knew that whatever was brewing between them right now was something she didn't want to end. She wanted to reclaim her singlehood in grand style. What better way than spending the night with a gorgeous man?

Hunter kissed her again, and she looped both of her arms around his neck and held on. His hand tightened on her waist, pulling her body against his. And the kiss deepened. Right there on the dance floor, they kissed as if they were the only two people in the room. It was the kind of display of public affection that would have had Lorraine rolling her eyes if she were witnessing it.

And yet, she'd been caught up in something spectacular with this man to the point where she was no longer thinking rationally. All she could think about was the fact that she didn't want their night to end.

Hunter was the one to break the kiss, but he didn't let her go.

He pressed his lips against her cheek, softly, and then moved his mouth to her ear. "You're absolutely beautiful," he told her. "You want to get out of here?"

"Yes," she said, and he kissed her again, a soft, lingering kiss that was both sweet and fiery. Lorraine nearly lost it. She could feel her entire body trembling from an overload of sensations. She wanted this man.

"If we're going to do this," she said, "then we should do this *now*."

He needed no further encouragement. He took her hand in his, linking their fingers, and led her back to her table, where her friends were looking at her with wide eyes and big smiles. It was as if they hadn't seen her with a man before!

Not one this fine…

Lorraine lifted the margarita she hadn't finished and downed it. "I'm leaving," she announced.

Rosa gaped at her. "What?"

"I…" She looked up at Hunter, and that smile… Oh, that smile. He pushed part of her veil over her shoulder, his fingers skimming her skin where her blouse scooped low at the back. She swallowed, then faced her friends again. "I'm going to call it a night. I hope you guys aren't mad."

"You're leaving with him?" Trina asked. Her eyes were dancing with delight.

"Yeah, uh, he'll take me home."

"I'll bet" was Amanda's mumbled comment.

Hunter tightened his arm around her waist, and Lorraine relaxed against him. "She's in good hands," he said.

"I'm sure she is," Trina said, her double meaning evident in the twinkle in her eyes.

"However," Rosa said, her expression becoming serious, "you never know what a serial killer looks like. So I'm going to give you my number so that you can call my phone right now. That way, I'll have your number. And I'll have a way to track my friend down—or evidence for the police—if she goes missing." Rosa batted her eyelashes, smiling sweetly. "You cool with that?"

Hunter chuckled. "Of course."

He took out his phone and called the number Rosa gave him. As her phone started to ring, she grinned. "Great. Now you can leave."

"I'm just going to go and say good-night to my buddies," Hunter said to Lorraine.

As he walked away, Rosa, Trina and Amanda began oohing and awwing. Amanda bit down on her knuckle as she shamelessly checked Hunter out.

"Oh. My. Word." Trina's eyes grew as wide as saucers. She fanned herself. "When… How?"

"He kind of came to my rescue outside of the restroom when some jerk was bothering me." Lorraine shrugged as though it was no big deal. Yet inwardly, her libido was doing jumping jacks. "The rest, as they say, is history."

"No, the rest is just beginning," Rosa said, beaming. She jumped to her feet and threw her arms around Lorraine. "Have fun, girl!"

"Don't do anything I wouldn't do," Trina added.

"In other words, do everything," Amanda said, and laughed.

"I'm entitled to do everything—I'm a married woman," Trina pointed out.

She was the only one of the group who was married now. Amanda and Rosa had never tied the knot.

Lorraine rounded the table to Trina and Amanda. "Okay, you guys," she said, extending her arms wide. They both got up, and she hugged them each in turn. "I love you both." She faced Rosa. "I love you all. Thanks again for coming out with me tonight. This has been a lot of fun."

"And it's about to get a lot better," Amanda said, giving her a knowing look.

Lorraine glanced in Hunter's direction and saw the moment he turned from his friends and met her gaze. He smiled, and as her heart skipped a beat, reality hit her.

She was leaving with this gorgeous man for a night that she knew would be incredible.

She couldn't wait.

Chapter 3

Lorraine's anticipation built as the taxi approached Hunter's place. They held hands, neither speaking. Her heart was racing. Was she really about to make love to this incredibly fine man?

They kept their hands off each other until they were in the elevator, where Hunter pulled her into his arms and started to kiss her. Lorraine gripped his biceps, her body melting against his. The elevator dinged, and they separated—barely—as they exited. Hunter led her down the hallway, then stopped in front of unit 1211. He quickly whisked her inside.

And then his mouth was on hers again, and delicious sensations exploded inside Lorraine's body like mini fireworks going off on the Fourth of July. His lips moved slowly, his breathing heavy. He nibbled gently on her bottom lip before suckling her flesh.

A breathy moan escaped her lips. She looped her arms around Hunter's neck.

"Oh, yeah," Hunter whispered. Then, tightening his hand on the base of her back, he swept his tongue into her mouth with one broad stroke.

Lorraine pressed her fingertips against Hunter's skin. Her desire was making her weak in the knees, light-headed.

He lifted her, and she fastened her legs around his body. Then he carried her down a hallway and through an open door.

It was the bedroom.

He took her straight to the bed, where he lowered their bodies down together, his on top of hers. He smoothed his hands up her side, his fingers flirting with her naked skin where her shirt had lifted. His touch was electric.

Hunter looked down at her. The room was dark, but pale light from outside filtered in through the slats in the blinds.

Lorraine smiled up at him and ran the tip of her heeled shoe down the length of his calf. Then she lifted her head to meet his lips and started kissing him again. She didn't want to talk. She only wanted to feel.

She pulled at the shirt tucked into his jeans until it was free, and then placed both palms on his naked back. His skin was warm, and those muscles… This man was the definition of fine. He shuddered a little as she ran her fingertips over his back in a circular motion, and Lorraine felt a surge of power. She lifted her hands higher and wrapped her legs tighter around him, reveling in feminine power.

Hunter also slipped his fingers beneath her shirt, and she sighed as they tantalized her skin. He kissed her jawline, moving his lips toward her ear, where he grazed her earlobe with his teeth. When he gently suckled it, she inhaled a sharp breath.

"You like that, do you?" Hunter asked.

"Very much."

"Let me ease back," he said softly. "I want to take your clothes off."

Had anyone ever said anything that turned her on more? She loosened her legs, and he stepped back. In the darkened room, she could still see the heat in his eyes as they roamed over her body. He then made quick work of unfastening her pants and shimmying them down her legs.

But she still wore her sexy pumps. Hunter lifted one foot in his hands and undid the buckle on her shoe, then tossed it onto the floor. He did the same with the other shoe, and then proceeded to take her jeans completely off her body.

For a moment, he stared down at her on the bed, then he lowered himself back over her, kissing her belly. The feel of his lips were so tender and sweet and made her body tingle with anticipation.

Hunter pushed her shirt up. His hands brushed against her nipples through her bra.

"Yes," she rasped. She hardly recognized this wanton woman she'd become.

He flicked the tip of his tongue over her stomach. "I love how you respond to me."

"I love how you're making me feel."

Hunter pulled at her bra until her breasts were exposed. He tweaked her nipples while continuing to kiss her belly, and Lorraine arched her back as delicious heat spread through her body like molten lava.

"Yes," she rasped.

Suddenly, Hunter slipped an arm beneath her and pulled her body against his. He was strong, sexy, virile. And every single touch of his was turning her on. He slipped his hand under her shirt and unfastened her bra, removing it from her body. Then he pulled her shirt over her head, and quickly discarded it in a heap on the floor.

His gaze moved from her face and down the length of her body. He let out a low whistle. "Mary, Mary, Mary."

Hearing the fake name shocked her slightly, but then she stopped thinking when Hunter stroked her inner thigh. He was doing just the right amount of teasing, drawing out the sexual chemistry between them. As Hunter's fingers went higher up her thigh, she let her legs fall apart. His mouth came down on hers as he stroked her most sensitive place through her underwear. She kissed him hungrily. His hands explored further, slipping beneath her panties to touch her sensitive flesh. He massaged and tantalized.

His mouth worked over hers while his fingers explored, driving Lorraine wild. Hunter was bringing her to heights

f pleasure she hadn't been to in forever. It felt amazing
to have a man touching her like this.

But she needed to touch him, too. She wanted to make
him feel the same kind of pleasure he was making her feel.
So she put both hands on his thighs. As he continued to
kiss her, she smoothed her hands up his legs, finally stroking his impressive shaft through his pants.

He moaned into her mouth.

"You have a condom?" she asked.

"I do."

A guy like him—of course had a condom. She could
imagine he had his pick of women wherever he went.

And tonight he'd picked her.

Without warning, he eased his body off hers and stood.
Cool air kissed her naked skin. She wanted him against
her, giving her warmth. When he began to unbutton his
shirt, all she could do was watch him. Watch as he did a
little striptease. He took off his shirt, revealing massive,
hot muscles and gorgeous skin. He had a spattering of
chest hair, the kind she would be happy to twirl her fingers through.

And he wasn't shy. Because when he tossed his shirt to
the floor and she gave a little cheer, he gyrated his hips as
though he were onstage performing for her. She laughed.

"You want to see more?" he asked.

"Oh, yeah…"

He unfastened the button on his jeans, unzipped them
and then began to drag them over his hips. He took his
time, continuing the striptease. Lorraine whistled when his
muscular thighs came into view. This man could grace the
cover of any magazine. He was that hot. And the more he
showed his playful side as well as his sexy side, the more
she wanted him.

Two could play at that game. She eased her hips up and
slipped her underwear off, and as her chest was pressed

against her leg she looked up at him and saw his eyes fastened to her body. He was waiting for her to sit back up and fully expose her nude body. So she gave him what he wanted, slowly sitting upright, then leaning back on her elbows. He got a small peek of her womanhood before she slowly crossed one leg over the other.

"You're killing me right now," Hunter said.

"You're killing me."

Hunter kicked his legs free of his jeans, and then slipped his briefs down his thighs. His erection sprang free. Lorraine's lips parted in awe. He was more impressive than she expected.

"The condom," she urged. "And hurry." It wasn't like her to be this bold, but if he didn't make love to her soon she was going to die. She needed him that badly.

He went to his side drawer and fished out a condom. As he took off the wrapper and began to put it on, Lorraine uncrossed her legs, exposing herself further. She heard his groan of delight as his eyes gobbled up the sight of her. Never had she felt more desired.

Hunter stalked toward the bed, all serious now. He lowered his head and captured her lips in a deep kiss. He urged her backward onto the bed, holding his weight off her with his strong arms.

He slipped a hand between their bodies and smoothed it over her belly. When he slid it up to her breast and he circled her nipple with a finger, Lorraine moaned into his mouth.

His lips quickly left hers in search of the nipple he had just teased, and he drew it deeply into his mouth. Lorraine gasped as Hunter suckled sweetly, his lips pulling, his tongue trilling.

This was heaven.

Hunter moved his mouth to her other nipple, and as

he did, his hands found her center again. She was ready for him.

More than ready.

He moved up her body and settled between her thighs. He guided his shaft slowly into her, making sure that he was in no way hurting her.

Lorraine gasped, overwhelmed with emotions.

"Are you okay?" he asked.

"I've never been more okay," she replied.

He filled her, and her eyelids fluttered shut. The feel of his strong body pressed against hers, between her thighs, inside her… Heat spread through her body like molten lava.

They started off slow, moving tentatively. Every time he burrowed deep inside her, Lorraine dug her fingers into his back.

"You like that?" he asked.

"Yes…"

He moved faster, picking up the pace. Lorraine arched her hips to meet his thrusts. His deep groans filled the air, mixing with her soft moans. She buried her face in his neck. The scent of his cologne flirted with her senses, and she gripped him harder. This man was irresistible with his superfine body. And tonight, he was hers.

She kissed his moist skin, then ran her tongue along his flesh. He tasted salty and sweet and delicious. He grunted, his body trembling against hers, making her heady with desire.

She matched his quickening movements, sighing with each of his thrusts. Their bodies slid against each other's as their coupling became hot and frenzied. Raw, carnal need consumed Lorraine with the ferocity of a raging fire.

Hunter locked his arms behind her knees and thrust deep. Lorraine moaned long and hard. "Oh, God," she uttered. "Again."

Hunter eased back, then once again burrowed himself deeply inside her. Lorraine gripped the bed sheets as heat pooled in her abdomen. Her limbs grew tauter, her climax near.

"Hunter…" Lorraine rasped.

He kissed her, his tongue delving into her mouth. The dual sensation of his lips pressed against hers and his shaft deep inside her sent prickles of pleasure all over her skin. Within seconds, the tension reached its peak and then began to unravel. Her limbs became like jelly as the heat spiraled from within her abdomen and out through the rest of her body. "Hunter… Oh, yes. Yes!"

And as Lorraine rode the wave of pleasure, she was transported from her old life to a new one. In Hunter's arms, she wiped the slate clean on her past and was initiated as a new woman.

Chapter 4

Lorraine's eyelids fluttered as she stirred and turned onto her side. As she did, the sheet covering her body slipped down over her hip. Cool air kissed her naked skin. She frowned slightly. She wasn't wearing her pajamas? Her thighs pressed together, and she felt another odd sensation: a dull ache. What the—

Her eyes popped open, taking in the darkness. It wasn't so dim that Lorraine couldn't see the tall armoire, the white leather chair in the corner. This was not her bedroom. Her heart began to thud.

It all came back to her, and dread filled her belly with the weight of a bowling ball. She remembered exactly where she was.

The bar. The sexy stranger. The drinking.

Her world being rocked.

Oh, God. Had she really just had a one-night stand?

As she lay in the bed, afraid to move, afraid to see the proof of what she'd done, the soft, steady sounds of breathing filled the air. Slowly, Lorraine turned her head to look on the other side of the bed. Her heart slammed against her rib cage when she saw the man beside her. Hunter. That was his name. And as she stared at him, she was momentarily distracted by that amazing body. The bed sheets covered him from the waist down, but that muscular chest, those wide shoulders and those washboard abs were gloriously exposed.

Heat pooled in her center. Oh, how that sexy body had

thrilled her last night. She had been shameless in her desire, clutching Hunter tightly as they'd made love, whispering in his ear just how to please her.

Her cheeks burned with the memory. She had to get out of here.

She inched her body to the edge of the bed, then glanced at Hunter. His lips were parted, his eyes closed, his chest rising and falling with deep breaths. The bed dipped as she slipped out of it, and thankfully, Hunter didn't stir. The room was dark, but her vision was adjusting. She scanned the room for her clothes. Her bra was on the hardwood floor beside the bed. A foot away was her shirt. Where was her underwear? She didn't see it.

She whirled her head around. Her jeans and underwear were on the far right of the bed close to Hunter's shirt. Lorraine cringed. In their haste to get naked, their clothes had landed anywhere and everywhere. That's how excited she had been to make love with a stranger.

Though she certainly couldn't call him a stranger after how well acquainted they had gotten last night...

She quickly scooped up all of her clothes and crept as quietly as she could across the cool floor toward the door. Last night had been amazing. Honestly, it had been just what she'd needed. Though leaving the bar with a man she didn't know was uncharacteristic of her, she didn't regret it, and she wasn't going to mentally berate herself for what she'd done.

The bedroom door was ajar, and she slowly edged it open wide enough that she could slip through. Once she was on the other side of it, she exhaled a breath she didn't realize she was holding. She glanced to the right. The hallway opened up to the living room. Though she desperately wanted to get out of here as quickly as possible, she had to use the bathroom. So she tiptoed to the left and tried the door there. It was the bathroom. Thank God.

She caught sight of her reflection. She looked…satis-ed. She couldn't help smiling. Her body was throbbing a places it hadn't throbbed in years.

The smile went flat as she started to make her way to he condo door. Her purse, her shoes. They were in the edroom.

"Damn it," she whispered, balling her hands into fists. he'd escaped, and now she had to go back in there?

She had no choice. Creeping slowly across the floor, he slipped back into the bedroom. Her stomach bottomed ut. Hunter was now on his side, no longer on his back. Was he awake?

Standing still, Lorraine stared at him for a good fifteen seconds. His breathing sounded even. He was still asleep.

She walked forward in search of her belongings. Her purse was at the foot of the leather chair. As she retrieved that, she scowled. Where were her shoes?

The memory of her jeans down around her ankles and Hunter's fingers brushing her skin as he removed her shoe hit her full force, and her cheeks flushed. She'd been on the right side of the bed. Her shoes *had* to be there somewhere.

She walked forward, noticing Hunter's jeans in a heap. Rosa was fond of saying, "If you can't find something you're looking for, most likely it's underneath something else."

Bingo!

Lorraine hurried over to the jeans and picked them up. *Yes!* She quickly claimed her shoes, then looked at Hunter to see if he had moved. He hadn't. Lorraine started for the bedroom door again.

Just before she exited, she stole one last glance at Hunter over her shoulder. The absurdity of the situation hit her, and she had to fight to hold in a laugh. Here she was try-ing to sneak away from a gorgeous guy who had given her the best pleasure of her life. She'd really won the lottery

in the hot-sex department. Instead of running, she shoul
be slipping back into his bed.

Lorraine walked out of the room. There would be n
round three. The two hot sessions had been amazing, an
Hunter had served his purpose. He'd left her sexually sated
and now she could move forward a new woman. She fel
a little bit bad about leaving him without saying goodbye
but she had no clue if he would want to exchange numbers and stay in touch. No, Lorraine didn't want to com-
plicate matters any further. It was best that she just leave
and avoid any awkward morning-after chatting.

The door's lock clicked, and in the silent condo it
sounded like a bomb going off. Her heart racing, Lorraine hurriedly opened the door and escaped into the hallway. She squinted, the bright lights assaulting her eyes.
Forget the elevator. She jogged barefoot to the stairwell.

Once she was there, she put her shoes on, then made her
way down the stairs to the building's first floor.

Lorraine straightened her spine and walked briskly toward the double glass front doors. She didn't give the se-
curity guard sitting at a desk even a cursory glance. Had
she seen him when they'd entered the building? Had he
seen her?

It didn't matter. So what if he knew how she'd spent the
last six hours? She wasn't the first woman to leave a man's
place in the middle of the night.

The cool night air enveloped her as she stepped outside. It was jarring. She opened her purse and withdrew
her phone. Then groaned when she found that it was dead.
At least she had a portable charger in her purse, so she
plugged her phone in. Standing there on the sidewalk, it
seemed to take forever to boot up. She hated that she had
to stay here any longer, but she needed to access her Uber
app in order to get a ride out of here.

Lorraine glanced over her shoulder. No one was there. Hunter wasn't coming after her.

The time on her phone read 4:03. As she accessed the Uber app, she realized she would need to stay at the address that was automatically sent to the driver. She didn't want to linger in front of Hunter's building, but what choice did she have? All she could do was wait—and pray that Hunter didn't come downstairs.

Hunter's eyelids popped open. In a nanosecond, a memory came flooding back. Soft breasts pressed against his chest, luscious lips suckling his skin.

The woman.

Mary.

A smile breaking out on his face, he glanced to the right. The smile went flat. Mary wasn't in his bed.

Easing his head up, he looked around the room. Nothing. He strained to hear any sounds coming from his en suite bathroom. There was no sound, no light emanating from beneath the bathroom door.

Where the heck was Mary?

Sitting up, he dragged a hand over his face. Then he chuckled, but the sound held no mirth. He'd been ditched.

How long had it been since that had happened? Not since his first year of college, and he certainly hadn't connected with that girl the way he'd connected with Mary.

Hunter scratched his head. His time with Mary had been spectacular. As welcomes to town went, it had been off the charts. So why had she taken off? It wasn't as if Hunter wanted a serious relationship with her—something that he knew that she, as a newly divorced woman, also didn't want. But a friends-with-benefits arrangement with a woman he connected with on such a carnal level? That would suit Hunter just fine. He'd liked Mary's spunk, her personality and the way that hot body of hers writhed beneath his.

Heat pooled in Hunter's groin. Just thinking about her was getting him aroused again. He closed his eyes, remembered the look of pleasure on her face as he'd made love to her, the way she'd dug her fingernails into his back. She'd likely left a mark or two.

A tingle of pleasure shot down his spine as he recalled those spectacular moments together. She'd wanted him— desperately. She wouldn't have ditched him.

Hunter stood. Maybe Mary had needed to leave, and he'd been sleeping like the dead after their intense love-making. His shoulders relaxed with that thought. Yes, that made sense. She was in a rush, didn't want to wake him, but she no doubt left him a note somewhere. Certainly Hunter couldn't be so delusional as to have imagined their amazing connection. Their chemistry had been sizzling, so why wouldn't she want more of that?

He didn't bother to slip into his briefs. He wanted to find the note she'd left. Naked, he wandered into his kitchen and then the living room looking for it. When he didn't find one, he returned to the bedroom and checked the night tables. Frowning, he scratched his head.

And then it hit him. The bathroom was likely the best place to leave a note. He had two of them. His en suite, and the main one.

Hunter went into the main bathroom first, and saw no note on the counter. Nothing on the edge of the bathtub. So he went back into his bathroom, but also found nothing there. He glanced into the mirror, saw the confusion etched on his face.

There had to be a note *somewhere*.

And then he started to laugh. Mary was making a game of this. Hadn't she displayed a playful side in the bar and in his bed? Of course she wasn't going to make this easy for him.

Hunter wandered back out to the condo at large and

checked the hall table. Then he went into the kitchen, his eyes sweeping over the counters. He moved from there to the small dining room table, but again he found nothing.

The living room. Something had to be there.

Hunter crossed into the living room, but a quick glance told him that there was no note on the coffee table. He walked over to the wall entertainment unit and perused the shelves there. Again, nothing.

Hunter turned, his eyes landing on the sofa. There was nothing there, but he strode over to it. He slipped his hands between the cushions.

"This is stupid," he said when he found nothing other than some cookie crumbs. "What am I doing?"

His ego was getting to him, clouding his judgment. But as reality dawned, the amusement inside him fizzled, much like a campfire flickering out. Mary *hadn't* left a slip of paper anywhere, not even a tissue with a smiley face and her phone number.

How stupid he had been to think that she'd been playing some kind of game with him. Instead, she'd simply played him.

Hunter's jaw clenched. There was no doubt about it. He'd been ditched.

Chapter 5

When Lorraine saw Rosa's number flashing on her phone's screen at 1:23 in the afternoon, she knew exactly why her friend was calling. She wanted the lowdown about what had happened last night.

Lorraine swiped the talk icon to answer the call. "Hello."

"How was it!" Rosa asked without preamble.

"How was what?" Lorraine replied, feigning innocence.

"You know very well what I'm asking about! You left the bar with one of the sexiest guys in Ocean City. Enquiring minds want to know what happened next. In minute-by-minute detail."

"Girl, are you actually calling to find out the dirty details of my night?"

"What kind of friend would I be if I didn't? By the way, I'm detecting a really happy tone in your voice. No, wait. Make that a *satisfied* tone."

Lorraine chuckled. "I did have a great night."

"Yes!" Rosa said. Then, "Wait, how great? A few kisses and a movie great? Or—"

"Let's just say it was *fan*tastic. Well beyond a few kisses. Honestly, a fabulous night." Sighing, Lorraine plopped herself backward on the pile of pillows on her bed. Yes, her reply had been exuberant, but who could blame her? It had been a long time since she'd had good sex—even as a married woman—and last night she'd scratched an itch that she'd been desperate to scratch.

On the other end of the line, Rosa squealed. "Oh, that's wonderful! Girl, you deserve it. Just one look at him and I knew he'd be a great lover. That body... Wow."

"I can't even begin to tell you how good it was," Lorraine gushed. "Our connection was unreal. We were so into each other... Or maybe it's just because it had been so long for me. But he seemed to enjoy our night as much as I did." Lorraine blushed, remembering just how ravenous she had been. *Yes, I like that. Ooh, touch me there.* A shiver of delight raced down her spine, and she sucked in a deep breath. "I probably gave him quite the workout! But, hey, he wasn't complaining."

"He sounds like just what you need," Rosa said. "When are you going to see him again?"

"See him again? Um, no," Lorraine said succinctly, shooting down that idea.

"What do you mean?" Rosa asked. "If you had such a great night, and had so much chemistry... Why wouldn't you want more of that? I say you need a lot of that to firmly put your ex in the rearview mirror. A guy to have on speed dial for those nights that you feel lonely."

"I'm barely out of my marriage. Free at last, as they say. The last thing I want to do is get tied down with some new guy."

"But..."

"Last night was fun, just what I needed. And who knows, if I run into Hunter again we might have another great night. But I'm not trying to get into anything regular with someone. I just needed... You know what they call it, a palate cleanser. I have no regrets."

Rosa made a sound of derision. "I don't understand that logic."

"All I really needed was to feel wanted, beautiful, and Hunter gave me that. Now I can move forward. Surely that makes sense."

"Not to me, but hey, it's your life."

"Come on," Lorraine said. "You know my life is in total flux right now. I've been so stressed with work that I had to take some time off. I'm finally ready to concentrate on pursuing my real dream."

Lorraine loved her job as a palliative care nurse, but seven years of that kind of work had started to wear on her. All of the patients admitted to the hospice where she worked were at death's door. She saw people at their worst in terms of suffering and prognosis. She saw them when there was no more hope. It was her job to help keep them comfortable until they passed. Lorraine always prayed that the patients she got close to would make a miraculous recovery, be able to survive against the odds. But it never happened. There were no happy endings, unless you counted a person going as peacefully as they could.

And unfortunately, Lorraine was never able to detach her emotions from her work. She always got close to the men, women and children in her care, and losing them hurt her every single time.

"I know," Rosa said. "And I'm proud that you've taken a leave. You were stressed in your marriage, at work. You definitely needed a break. That's why I think you should keep someone like Hunter around to…perk your spirits… when the need arises."

"Sex can't solve everything," Lorraine said. "I had a great night, but today I'm a little down. You remember that older gentleman I told you about I was caring for?"

"The one who had no family visiting him?"

"That's the one. He passed away earlier this week, on Monday."

"Oh, Lorraine. I'm so sorry."

"I know I shouldn't let it affect me. I know the reality of what's going to happen when patients come in. My co-workers all remind me that I'm supposed to stay detached but pleasant. Don't get emotionally connected. But how do you really do that? And this man, he had no one. I'd gotten especially close to him. I couldn't help wondering why he had no family visiting, because he talked about them. He had regrets, talked about pushing his family away." Lorraine swallowed, remembering how Douglas's eyes had teared up when he'd talked about his son. "I wish I could detach myself from my patients, but I can't."

"You care. That's who you are. But when you care, there's always pain."

"Tell me about it. Anyway, his death really reinforced my desire to get out of palliative care and be on the other end of the health care spectrum. Help people when I can make a difference."

"But you did make a difference with him," Rosa said. "When he had no one, you were there for him. He didn't die alone."

"Thank you for saying that," Lorraine said, a swell of emotion rising in her chest. It did do her some good to think that her caring attitude comforted her patients in their time of emotional need. And it was true, Douglas Holland's eyes had lit up every time she visited with him. She would sit at his bedside and talk to him, push him in a wheelchair to the facility's courtyard so he could bask in the sunlight. She would read to him, which had been one of his favorite things. It was hard to believe that he was gone, even though she'd known he was dying.

"But I can only imagine how hard it is for you," Rosa said. "Caring for your patients, then losing them."

"Exactly," Lorraine said. "Anyway, get this. Yesterday morning, I got a call from his lawyer. He said he wants to meet me Monday morning for the reading of the will?" Lorraine's voice ended on a questioning note, because it was still so surreal to her.

"You're kidding."

"No, I'm not. It was the last thing I expected, and I'm still not sure how to process the news."

"Why didn't you mention it yesterday?"

"Because I'm still in shock," Lorraine answered. "This has never happened to me before. Besides, I didn't want to bring anyone down—including myself—with talk about his death."

"What do you think he left you?"

"I have no clue. When I got the call from the lawyer, I was floored. Reading of the will sounds so official. I didn't get the impression that he was loaded or anything. Just an average guy of average means."

"What if he left you a million dollars?"

"Girl, you're crazy," Lorraine said.

"But what if he did? You never know."

"I do know. If he had that kind of money, at least some of his family would have been around. A rich man who's dying and has to leave his fortune with someone? Even if they hated him, the family would have been there, making nice."

"You've got a point," Rosa said. "Yeah, you're probably right. And here I was, already planning a shopping spree! Just kidding."

Lorraine rolled her eyes. "Rosa, you're so silly."

"So, are you going to go?"

"I'm not sure," Lorraine said. "I'm debating it. I'm not his family, so in a way it doesn't feel right. Then I thought about some of the conversations I've had with some family members who fight about a will. I always point out that everyone needs to respect the deceased person's wishes. So I'd be a hypocrite if I didn't do the same. I'm sure he just wanted to leave me something small to show his gratitude." Lorraine pursed her lips, weighing her dilemma once again in her mind. One minute she convinced herself she shouldn't go to the meeting, the next she convinced herself she should. Right now, she was feeling pretty positive about the decision to attend the meeting. Shouldn't she respect Douglas's wishes?

"I guess I'll go," she said. "I'll respectfully accept whatever Douglas has left for me. Like I said, I'm sure it's something small but meaningful."

"It would be nice to have a keepsake from him," Rosa said. "I know he meant a lot to you."

"He really did." Lorraine's chest filled with warmth as she thought of him. Douglas was one person she'd remember for a long time.

"Someone else could mean a lot to you," Rosa all but sang. "Your hot new fling."

"Rosa, you're crazy," Lorraine protested. "That was one night, and it was great. But it won't be happening again."

The alarm sounded at Station Two. "Pump truck two, ladder truck two. Structure fire, 413 Fulmar way."

Forks and knives clanked against plates as Hunter and his fellow firefighters, who were seated at the dining hall table for breakfast, promptly dropped their cutlery and jumped up from their seats. They rushed to get into their turnout gear.

"This is it," Captain Mason Foley said to him. "Time to see what you're made of."

Hunter chuckled as he looked at Mason. He'd developed an easy camaraderie with him as he had with all the firefighters here. "Yep," Hunter said. "Let's do this."

As Hunter got into his turnout gear, his body reacted the way it always did when heading out to a call. His heart pounded and his pulse raced, his adrenaline flowing.

Today there was an additional sensation. His stomach was flexing. Mason had been joking, but he'd summed up Hunter's feelings. After arriving in Ocean City and securing his place with the fire service here, this was Hunter's first day on the job. An hour into his first shift and he was heading out to his first fire. He wanted to prove to the guys here that he was a good firefighter.

Within sixty seconds, all the firefighters were in their bunker gear, something they were trained to do. Time was of the essence when responding to a fire or any other emergency.

Peter, another firefighter, patted Hunter on the back once they were all seated in the rear of the pump truck. "Ready to rock and roll?"

"Oh, yeah," Hunter said.

The truck started off, jerking them all slightly to the right as it rounded the corner out of the firehouse bay. Tyler, who was driving, started the siren. Hunter looked out at the view of Ocean City as the truck moved rapidly down the street. This truly was a beautiful place. Unlike the dry desert of Nevada, Ocean City was lush and green. Lots of palm trees and thick green lawns and colorful flowers. Plus the view of the ocean never got old.

Sixteen years. Had it really been that long since he'd been here? When he'd left, he had seen Ocean City only as a place of despair and heartache. The place that had robbed him of his mother and twin sister. The place where his father had become emotionally distant. The fresh start in Reno had seemed the only thing to do for his sanity.

The truck headed up Cline Avenue, ascending the hillside. Hunter stared out at the small, colorful houses. Pale blue, yellow, green, some pink. This part of Ocean City had homes that were more like cottages and reminded him of the vibrant, colorful houses in the Caribbean. It was very picturesque.

Though Ocean City had a fairly large population, it had a small-town feel, with lots of diverse communities. There were neighborhoods like this, filled with young families and young professionals. Then there were the college students who populated the west side of the downtown area. There was an arts scene, and a vibrant night life. And yet the town never lost its charm. It felt warm and welcoming no matter where you went.

"So what happened to the woman at the bar you met a couple nights ago?" Peter asked. Hunter had been out with Omar, Tyler, Mason, Peter and a bunch of the other guys on their shift the night he'd met Mary. They'd taken him out to get him acquainted with all of his colleagues, to welcome him back to Ocean City and to Fire Station Two. He'd ditched them all once the opportunity to leave with Mary had presented itself, and their hooting, hollering and high fives had shown him that he had their approval. He'd felt kind of silly bailing on them, but there was something about Mary and leaving with her had been an opportunity he definitely couldn't pass up.

This morning, Hunter had avoided answering their questions when they'd sat down to start eating, but now that he was in the back of a moving truck with nowhere to go, Peter broached the subject again.

"Let's just put it this way," Hunter began, "it was a great welcome to Ocean City."

Peter fist-bumped him in congratulations. "That's what I'm talking about!"

"Ever going to see her again?" Omar asked.

Peter roared with laughter. "What are you trying to do, see him married off already?" He turned to Hunter. "Omar used to be our resident playboy. Until he off and fell in love."

"Love is the last thing on my mind," Hunter said.

"A man after my own heart," Peter said.

Even if Hunter were looking for love, it wasn't going to happen with Mary—not after the way she'd ditched him. He doubted he was ever going to see her again. He had her friend's number, but calling to track her down would seem desperate. If she wanted a one-night fling, so be it. He'd had a great time.

"The guys here keep dropping like flies," Peter went on. "Mason, Tyler and the one who shocked us all, Omar. At least now I have someone to hit the bars with. It's like there's some sort of disease spreading through our station… Forget the flu bug, this time it's the love bug."

"Yeah, yeah," Tyler said, glancing back at them from behind the wheel. "Peter, you only wish you could find yourself a woman who wanted to see you for more than a day."

All the guys laughed, but the laughter quickly faded when the billowing smoke from the structure fire came into view.

"There it is," Hunter said.

The pump truck came to a stop. No more joking, they started affixing their helmets and masks.

"That's thick black smoke," Mason said.

"The building needs to be ventilated," Hunter added. No one could go into a building with dense hot smoke without an outlet for the fire to escape. Rapid reintroduction of oxygen could cause the building to blow.

In other words, a back draft. Back drafts had claimed the lives of many a firefighter.

"Is anyone in the building?" the chief was asking the crowd of onlookers when Hunter and the rest of the guys jumped off the truck.

"No," a woman said. She was barefoot, wearing a robe, and her blond hair was disheveled. "My husband and I smelled smoke, so we ran out. It's just the two of us."

The chief quickly assessed the fire. "Richards, Lovett— get that ladder on the roof. Take an ax and start ventilation. Wickham and Rogers, get to the back of the building and do the same."

The men he'd named sprang into action. Omar and

Hunter worked at getting the hoses. Tyler went to the pump truck's controls.

Flames shot through the roof when the two firefighters there put a hole in it. Richards jerked backward, almost falling off the ladder as he tried to escape the sudden burst of flame. A collective gasp erupted in the crowd. Once Richards regained his footing on the ladder, people began to clap.

"Wickham, Rogers," the chief said into the walkie-talkie affixed to his jacket. "How's it looking back there?"

"Window's open now," one of them responded. "This one's burning real hot."

"Holland," the chief said to Hunter, addressing him by his surname.

"Yes, Chief?"

"You and Ewing get a hose around to the back, start fighting that fire."

"Yes, sir." Hunter and Omar lifted a heavy hose onto their shoulders, the two of them carrying it to the back of the building. Hunter hit the nozzle to release the water, and the hose jerked backward from the pressure as he did. They immediately began attacking the angry flames shooting through the smashed open window. It felt good being back on the job. Hunter had missed this. The adrenaline rush of fighting a fire that wanted to destroy and take as many casualties as possible.

Not if Hunter could help it.

More firefighters arrived from another firehouse, and together everyone attacked the flames. The smoke turned from black to white as it mixed with moisture and rose into the air in a giant plume.

Red angry flames reached through the broken window like tentacles trying to claw at them. Hunter held on to the taut hose and aimed, blasting the fire. "I don't think so."

And when the flames began to recede, replaced with

more white smoke, satisfaction filled him. Oh, yeah, it definitely felt good to be back in action. And at least while he was fighting this fire, he wasn't thinking about the woman who'd left him overheated in his bed, wanting more.

Chapter 6

On Monday morning, Lorraine whipped her car into an empty parking spot just a block down from the building that housed the lawyer's office. She got out and put enough money in the meter for two hours. Then she glanced at her cell phone. She'd made good time. She had ten minutes to spare before her appointment.

She walked briskly toward the tall gray-bricked building. She sucked in a nervous breath before pushing through the revolving doors.

The lawyer had given her specific instructions, so she knew she was going to the third floor, then turning right to head to suite 309. She passed well-dressed people moving swiftly across the floor. Places to go, people to see. Lorraine's heels clicked against the marble, seeming to accentuate the rapid beating of her heart.

She glanced at the people around her. Slick business suits, pencil skirts, blazers. They looked like executives or other serious business types. Lorraine swallowed. Should she have worn a suit as opposed to the floral skirt and cotton blouse she'd chosen?

She reached the bank of elevators and stared at her reflection in the polished metal doors. Why was she doubting herself? She looked perfectly acceptable. After all, she wasn't here to apply for a job. She was here for a meeting. It was just her nerves getting to her. Meeting with a lawyer about a will was so official.

Yesterday, she'd decided to come here. Today, she

couldn't shake the tightening in her belly at the idea of seeing Douglas's family. Surely they would be here. Would they be angry to see a stranger at what they'd understandably expect to be a private family meeting? And would they give her a hard time regarding whatever had been left to her?

The elevator doors opened, and Lorraine's palms started to sweat. Everyone waiting piled on, but she didn't move.

"You coming?" a man asked. He held his arm across the elevator doors to prevent them from closing.

Lorraine straightened her spine and forced a smile. "Yes."

She walked onto the elevator. Someone had already pressed the button for the third floor, so she stood and waited for it to ascend. Depending on how things played out in the meeting, if Douglas left her something significant and the family objected, she wouldn't fight with them to keep whatever he'd intended for her to have. She hated family quarrels like this over material things, and she didn't want to be a part of one. Though on a personal note, she wouldn't mind giving Douglas's family members a piece of her mind. Where had they been when their father, brother or whoever he was to them had been suffering and dying?

The elevator landed on the third floor. Lorraine inhaled a deep breath, then stepped off. She saw suite 309 immediately. It was the office directly to the right of the elevator. It boasted a large frosted-glass window pane and double doors. The name of the firm was inscribed in the glass to the left of the doors, and made quite the impression. It was certainly a more elaborate office than she'd expected, the kind of law office that Lorraine imagined people with substantial money would use.

She pulled open the right-side door, finding it heavy. Inside, there was a large silver desk structure to the left and chairs on the opposite wall, where three people currently sat, waiting. The receptionist, a young woman with an olive complexion and a full mane of curly black hair, smiled at her instantly.

Lorraine looked at the wall clock behind the reception desk. She had five minutes until the appointment. Perfect. She'd timed it so that she would arrive at the lawyer's office just in time for the meeting. She didn't want to linger in the waiting room and possibly see Douglas's family members, who might have questions for her.

Lorraine made her way over to the reception desk. "Hello," she said to the receptionist. "I'm here to meet with Joseph Finkel."

"Are you Lorraine Baxter?"

"Yes, I am."

The receptionist got to her feet. "Follow me. They're ready for you."

Lorraine's stomach flip-flopped. *They're.* Just how many people were in the meeting? One? Two? A small army? Again, she wondered if she should have told the lawyer that she wasn't interested in whatever Douglas wanted to leave her.

Why are you so nervous about this? she asked herself as she followed the receptionist. But she knew why. She was fearing the worst. She'd seen far too many family members fight about assets right after a loved one had passed, and often even right in front of the dying person lying helpless on a bed.

The receptionist stopped in front of mahogany double doors at the end of the hallway. Etched into a gold plate on the door was the word Boardroom. The receptionist opened the right side of the door and stepped beyond the threshold. "Mr. Finkel, Lorraine Baxter."

There was a middle-aged, dark-haired man at the end of the boardroom table near the door, and he immediately stood. "Thank you, Lucia," the man said, then smiled in Lorraine's direction.

Lucia retreated down the hallway, and Joseph walked toward Lorraine. Extending his hand, he said, "Hello, Lorraine."

Planting a smile on her face, hoping to hide her nervousness, she approached the lawyer and shook his hand. "Nice to meet you," she said.

"Nice to meet you, as well."

Lorraine's eyes wandered around the room, and she saw that there was only one other person at the table. A man sitting just to the left of the lawyer's seat with his back facing her.

"Is this everyone?" Lorraine asked.

"Yes. It's just the two of you."

The man shifted in his seat to face her, and her eyes locked with his.

Lorraine reeled backward, losing her footing. Her lips parted on a silent gasp. Her stomach flinched violently, as though she'd just been sucker punched.

Oh, no... Oh, God, please...

His eyes widened, registering shock, and his face contorted. Then something else flashed on his face. Something akin to anger.

This can't be happening! Lorraine's heart began to pound so hard she could hear it thundering in her ears. She stood paralyzed as the lawyer released her hand.

Joseph Finkel gestured to the available chair on his right. "Please, have a seat."

Lorraine didn't move.

"Don't be shy," the lawyer teased. His tone was lighthearted, and he was clearly trying to alleviate her nerves. But he didn't understand. He had no clue.

Lorraine tried to swallow, but her throat was suddenly

dry. She began to walk across the room, unable to take her eyes off Hunter. He was holding her gaze, glaring at her.

Lorraine pulled her chair out and sat. "This is the only family?" she asked, her voice hoarse.

"You two are the only beneficiaries named in the will," the lawyer explained. "Lorraine, this is Douglas Holland's son, Hunter." The lawyer looked in Hunter's direction. "Hunter, this is Lorraine Baxter."

Hunter merely nodded, but didn't reach across the table to shake her hand. It was just as well. The last time he'd touched her, his hands had been giving her body immense pleasure, and his eyes had been smoky with desire. Now, he was looking at her with contempt.

Was this really happening? Or was Lorraine in the middle of a nightmare?

The very man she'd slept with—the man who'd rocked her world—was sitting across the table from her. How was this possible?

Suddenly, Hunter was standing, his large, athletic body looming over the table. Lorraine sucked in a sharp breath and leaned backward in her chair. But what did she expect him to do? Reach across the table and throttle her?

"*Lorraine*, is it?" He seemed to rub in the name, and may as well have added, "Liar."

In hindsight, giving him a false name had been silly and unnecessary. But was it really that big of a deal? It wasn't as if she'd planned to see him again. It would be a moot point if not for the fact that he was here right now, somehow back in her life.

"Yes," Lorraine croaked.

Hunter stretched his muscular body across the table and extended his hand. His pale blue dress shirt strained against his well-honed biceps. Despite the situation, Lorraine couldn't help checking out that fine form. He was gorgeous. Sexy.

A stallion in the bedroom.

God help her, this really was happening. Lorraine wanted to wither away and die.

"You don't want to shake my hand?" Hunter asked, a challenge.

"Of course." Lorraine wiped her palms against her skirt. "My hands are just a bit sweaty."

Trying her best to give him a level, nonchalant gaze, she lifted a hand and accepted his. She felt a zap of electricity as it enveloped hers.

"Nice to meet you," Hunter said. His words were innocent enough, but the look in his eyes was anything but. The tight set of his lips and the tautness of his jaw made it clear that he was barely keeping his anger under control. Was the lawyer picking up on any of the undercurrent of tension between them?

Lorraine was finally able to swallow. "Nice to meet you, as well," she said, her voice sounding as if she had a frog in her throat. She quickly glanced away.

She tried to pull her hand back, but he didn't immediately release it. Her gaze flew to his again, and he flashed her a knowing look. Only then did he loosen his grip, and Lorraine pulled her hand back. Her palm was sweaty, her heart beating fast.

Did Hunter's anger stem from the fact that she'd walked out on him, or because he was shocked to see her here? His father had left her something in his will. She could only imagine the suspicious thoughts going through his mind.

"There's no need to be worried or nervous," Joseph Finkel said to her. "This time a trip to the lawyer's office means a good thing."

Obviously, she looked and sounded like a nervous wreck, to the point where the lawyer had to reassure her that she wasn't about to be sued for millions of dollars.

Joseph tapped the folder in front of him and said, "All

right, let's get started. You are both here today for the reading of Douglas Holland's will. Hunter, as I was telling you before, Lorraine was a nurse at the hospice where your father resided before his death."

Lorraine glanced at Hunter, saw that he was staring at her. In fact, she knew he hadn't stopped staring at her. She could feel his gaze burning her skin.

"His nurse, yes," Hunter said, his voice monotone. "Interesting."

"Are there no other family members coming?" Lorraine asked the lawyer—anything to keep from concentrating on Hunter. Oh, shoot. She'd already asked that, hadn't she?

"No. Hunter is Douglas's only family member named in the will."

The lawyer must have thought she was a dimwit. Still, she pressed on, more to avoid talking to Hunter than anything else. "And he didn't want to leave everything to his son?"

Why, oh why hadn't she told the lawyer's secretary that she didn't want whatever had been left for her in the will? Why had she agreed to come to this meeting? Her cheeks were burning and her chest was tight. All she wanted now was to flee.

"Apparently, you made quite the impression on my father," Hunter commented dryly, and the look he gave Lorraine had her thinking that he was really speaking about the impression she'd made on *him* during their night together.

"Douglas Holland didn't have much family left," Joseph explained. "His wife died some years back, and a daughter passed away when she was young. So Hunter's the only immediate family he had. There were other family members, but he was estranged from them. If you're concerned that someone else might come forward to contest the will, you needn't be."

Oh, good Lord. That's the last thing she wanted Hunter thinking. That her concern was for herself and no one contesting what Douglas had left her. "Actually, I'm just... curious. Most people have more than one family member."

"I understand that you're surprised. Maybe even questioning why you'd be included in the will." Joseph smiled. "Douglas was adamant about changing his will to include you. He told me that during his last days, you were like family to him, Lorraine."

Lorraine glanced Hunter's way. She felt as though she were some sort of specimen under a microscope the way he was looking at her.

"You greatly impacted his life in a positive way," Joseph went on. "He specifically told me that you made him feel so much better about facing death and brought some purpose and meaning to his life."

"He said that?" Lorraine asked, her forehead scrunching as she looked at the lawyer.

"Yes."

Tears sprang to her eyes as a wave of emotion washed over her. "Thank you for telling me that," Lorraine said. She dabbed at her eyes with her fingertip. "That means a lot."

Then she glanced at Hunter, caught the none-too-subtle eye roll.

"He really appreciated you," Joseph said. "Felt you went above and beyond with him."

"I did what any nurse would do," Lorraine said, wishing that her voice wasn't so stilted. If only Hunter wasn't sitting across from her. Any other person, and she could get through this.

"Your modesty is exactly what he found endearing," Joseph said.

"Just how close were you to my father?" Hunter demanded.

At the question, Lorraine's eyes flew to his. He raised an eyebrow, and she got instantly what he was trying to imply. Her stomach bottomed out. The mere idea was horrifying.

"We spent a lot of time talking," she said tersely. "I read him books. He loved mysteries. I used to help him walk outside with his walker. When he was too weak to walk, I took him outside in his wheelchair. He loved feeling the sun on his skin." Lorraine met Hunter's hard gaze and quickly kept speaking. "He was alone. No family ever came to visit." Now she was the one to give Hunter a pointed look. "I felt bad for him."

"I was in Nevada," Hunter quickly said, the defensiveness in his tone clear. "And heck, I didn't even know he was dying."

"I'm not making a judgment against you. I'm just explaining." But Lorraine wasn't being entirely truthful. Hunter hadn't been in touch with his father enough to know that the man was dying. What answer could be good enough to explain that?

But she wasn't about to mention that to him, because she didn't want to irritate him. She wanted to get out of this meeting unscathed and move forward with her life.

"I was there for your father because it broke my heart to see him sad and alone," Lorraine continued. "It's very hard, working in a hospice. People are understandably depressed. I do whatever I can to help brighten their day."

"I'll bet you're great at that."

Lorraine's cheeks burned, and she only hoped that her pale skin wasn't red enough for the lawyer to notice that she was blushing violently. Hunter's meaning was clear. What did he think she was? Some kind of woman who slept with random men from a bar *and* her dying patients? A vixen trying to dupe his dad into including her in the will?

"A regular Little Miss Sunshine," he mumbled.

Lorraine's back stiffened. She glanced at the lawyer, but he was flipping through the pages in front of him and seemed oblivious to Hunter's verbal assault.

Lorraine needed to get out of here. She'd made a horrible mistake coming to this meeting. She cleared her throat, then spoke. "You know, I came to this meeting because I felt it was the right thing to do out of respect for Mr. Holland. However, sitting here it's just hit me that it's inappropriate for me to be here. I'm not his family. I have no desire to receive any gift from him. Whatever he intended for me should go to his son."

Lorraine pushed her chair back and stood. She secured her purse under her arm.

"Hold on," Joseph said before she could take a step. "Please, sit. I realize this may be uncomfortable for you— that's perfectly normal. Especially when you didn't expect it, and when—as you say—there's a family member who's a rightful heir. But let me allay any concerns. First of all, Hunter is not questioning—nor contesting—his father's will. I explained who you were and that Douglas wanted to honor you in his will, and Hunter seemed quite happy that someone had brought some comfort and peace into his father's life during his final days." The lawyer looked at Hunter, nodding, as if to solicit an affirmative response from him. Though Hunter's lips were pulled tightly together, he did nod.

Joseph smiled kindly at Lorraine. "I suppose you've never been to one of these before. You seem extra nervous. I just want to assure you that this is standard, and you're going to be very happy at the end of this meeting."

That was impossible! She might just have a heart attack before this meeting was over!

Nonetheless, Lorraine slithered into her seat again.

"Anyway," the lawyer continued, "let's get right to it. Douglas Holland had a personal home, and the house is be left to his son." He flipped through some of the papers in his folder. "He also had two rental properties. One of them, however, is currently co-owned with his brother, Damien, with whom he was estranged. There is a current legal dispute initiated by Damien regarding one of the properties, however. We can discuss that later, Hunter, but essentially your uncle claims money is owed to him."

Hunter nodded.

"He had a portfolio of stocks and bonds," Joseph continued. "These are the documents…"

Lorraine tuned out the lawyer's voice as he went through stocks and bonds. She heard something about a pickup truck and other assets all bequeathed to Hunter. In fact, it seemed as though all of the assets were being left to Douglas's son, and rightly so. Why was Lorraine even here?

"And lastly," the lawyer said and faced her, "Mr. Holland has left you a store."

Lorraine's head shot up, then she narrowed her eyes. "Excuse me?"

"Apparently, you spoke to him about your desire to open a health food store and hopefully a medical clinic. He was moved by your vision to help people *before* disease strikes, and provide nutritional advice that can possibly offset disease. He absolutely wanted to help you achieve this dream. So, to that end, he purchased a store for you on Keele Street, 1437 Keele Street, to be exact. The building is currently vacant, so it's ready for you to start working on it. He also left money for you to do the required renovations."

Lorraine's eyes blurred as she stared at the lawyer. She blinked, trying to get him into focus, but he remained a haze. "I'm sorry. I—I—" She couldn't form coherent words.

"Wait a minute," Hunter said. "My father left her a *store*?"

Lorraine didn't look at him. She was trying to process

what she'd heard. Douglas had bought her a store? Fre
and clear?

"Are you sure?" she asked.

Joseph smiled at her. "Absolutely." He produced a folde
sheet of paper from the folder and passed it to her. "This i
the floor plan. The building is twenty-six hundred square
feet, so it's quite spacious."

Lorraine unfolded the paper. The floor plan was a rect-
angular shape, longer than it was wide. But it would give
her lots of room to put shelves for products, and to have
an office at the back where she could have a dietician
working.

"I…" She looked at the lawyer. "I own this?"

"There are documents that you'll need to sign to transfer
the ownership from his name, but, yes. I wanted him to set
this up differently before he passed, but he really wanted
this to be a surprise for you. He said—and I quote—'I
know she'll be sad when I die, and I want this gift to put
a smile on her face.' There's even money to take care of
the taxes."

Lorraine sucked in a sharp breath, her head swimming.
She gripped the edge of the table. She couldn't believe
this news.

"I—I need to sign this today?" To her own ears, Lorraine sounded as though she was confirming whether or
not she was going to be beheaded.

"I have a number for the real estate lawyer you'll need
to deal with. Pierce Muldoon. His office is in this building on the fifth floor. So, no, you don't have to sign the
paperwork immediately. Please feel free to review it. But
you do get to have the key now along with the legal papers." He placed the key on top of a manila envelope with
the paperwork and slid the envelope across the table to
her. "You're welcome to check out the property before you

contact Pierce, but effectively the store is yours. Signing the paperwork will make it official."

This was all so overwhelming. Lorraine glanced at Hunter before meeting the lawyer's gaze again. "So you're saying this is a done deal? Finalized?"

"Everything, even all the legal costs associated with the transfer of title. All you have to do is sign the paperwork. Whenever you're ready. I understand that it's a lot to take in."

Lorraine lifted the key and held it between her fingers, the metal cool against her skin. Was this really happening? This key would unlock her dream, a dream that Douglas believed in. Warmth filled her heart. It was wonderful knowing that he'd cared so much. Maybe she could do this. To honor Douglas, to—

She glanced at Hunter, and her heart stopped. His jaw was tight, his eyes narrowed. His disapproval was clear. How could she accept this gift?

Lorraine looked away and cleared her throat. "Pierce Muldoon," she said, reading the name on the card that was attached to the envelope with a paper clip.

"He's expecting your call."

Lorraine nodded. "Am I free to leave now? There's nothing else?"

"That concludes the meeting, yes," Joseph said. "Do you have any questions for me?"

"No, nothing. Not right now." Lorraine pushed her chair back and stood hastily. "Honestly, I just need some time to process this. It's so unexpected. Overwhelming. I'm sure you probably have business with Douglas's son, so I'll just leave so that you two can speak in private."

The lawyer gave her an odd look. She could only imagine that other people who'd been bequeathed substantial gifts in this office expressed jubilation. But she wasn't most people. And especially not in this situation…

How was Hunter Douglas's son? She was embarrassed seeing him here like this after their hot night together, but she didn't appreciate his attitude toward her. How dare he be so harsh with her when he hadn't been there for his father in his final hours? What a jerk.

"If you have any questions, please, don't hesitate to call. If you want to discuss anything with me before calling Pierce, I'm happy to answer any questions."

"Absolutely." Lorraine palmed the key and lifted the envelope with her other hand. "Thank you," she said, then abruptly started for the boardroom exit. Somehow, she managed not to sprint. Barely.

Until she was safely in the hallway. Then she took off, as if the very devil were chasing her.

Chapter 7

Hunter watched Lorraine leave. The way she jerked out of her chair so quickly and damn near tripped over her feet as she hurried to the exit, she was acting like a guilty woman trying to flee a crime scene.

The crime in this case—manipulating a vulnerable, dying man.

Why else would Hunter's father leave her in his will, and such a significant gift at that? Just because she'd talked with him and pushed him outside in the sunlight?

It wasn't that Hunter wanted that asset for himself. It was the idea that his father had likely been deceived when he'd been at his weakest point. In some part of his subconscious, he knew that he was focusing on his anger toward Lorraine in order to help push away his own nagging feelings of guilt.

Hunter heard the lawyer's voice, but his words sounded garbled to him. Suddenly, the depth of Lorraine's deception hit him full force.

She'd given him a fake name. Because she'd known who he was all along? Was that night in the bar some sort of twisted game for her? Convince a dying man to leave her in his will, then bed his son?

Though the concept sounded incredible, Hunter went with it. He wouldn't put it past her. After all, some people were insane. They got off on exactly this kind of subterfuge. Maybe she hated men, and this was some sort of inside joke for her. A way for her to stick it to the opposite sex.

If she'd had nothing to hide, why give him a fake name? He curled his hands into fists. Yes, the true picture of Lorraine was coming together in his mind, like a painting being revealed. She had duped his father *and* him. Why else would she make love with him and then take off?

"Hunter?"

The firm tone of the lawyer's voice penetrated his subconscious. Hunter quickly met the man's curious gaze. "Sorry. What were you saying?"

"She did seem quite overwhelmed, didn't she?" Joseph asked, clearly assuming that Hunter was deep in thought over Lorraine.

"Very," Hunter said. "Makes me wonder why."

"She was probably worried that you were going to be upset with her. Possibly object to the property your father left to her. You can't begin to imagine the amount of squabbles I have to deal with in this office between family members, let alone someone who's *not* a part of the family. And in your case, because you're strangers—I can understand her wariness."

Heat clawed at Hunter's throat. *Strangers.* That word was no longer appropriate. He and Lorraine had become very familiar with each other's bodies, with every erogenous zone.

"Are you upset about this?" Joseph asked.

"I'm…confused," Hunter answered honestly.

"Any questions you have, ask. I can give you perspective on what your father was thinking, allay any fears about his frame of mind."

Oh, yes, Hunter had questions. But the truth was, the person with the answers was the woman who'd just left the boardroom. Hunter pushed his chair back and stood. "Give me a moment? I'll be back in five."

"If you're planning to go talk to Lorraine, I have to advise against—"

But Hunter was already out of the boardroom. He darted down the hallway.

As he stepped into the reception area, he could see out to the bank of elevators through a clear sliver in the frosted glass. The hem of Lorraine's skirt disappeared into the elevator.

Hunter hurried out of the office, but the elevator closed just as he reached it.

"Damn," he uttered. Then he spun around, his eyes searching for the exit sign. Quickly spotting it, he headed in the direction indicated, down the hallway. He pushed open the door to the stairwell and raced below, hoping to get to the first floor when the elevator did.

His dress shoes skidded on the first floor landing, but he didn't break stride. He pulled open the door that led to the building's main floor foyer. His eyes flitted from left to right as he raced toward the bank of elevators.

That's when he saw her. She was pushing through the revolving door leading to the street.

Hunter quickly changed direction and charged after her. There were more people going through the door, so he made the split second decision to use the manual one to its right.

Lorraine was walking toward the left, her gait noticeably more relaxed. "Lorraine," he called.

She stopped dead in her tracks, as if momentarily paralyzed by his voice. And then she shot a glance over her shoulder, her eyes filled with worry. The worry turned to fear when her gaze connected with his. Turning, she quickly started down the street.

"Oh, no, you don't," Hunter mumbled, and he immediately gave chase.

Lorraine started to run, and a second later, the manila

envelope and her purse fell from under her arm. Her frustrated outburst was none too subtle. She bent to scoop up her belongings, but she would never be able to escape him fast enough now.

Hunter dropped on to his haunches and picked up the envelope as she scooped up a lipstick and compact that had spilled from her purse. Lorraine's wide eyes met his, full of panic. Something inside of him clenched. He didn't like her looking at him like that, as though she was afraid of him.

But she did owe him some answers, and he intended to get them. Trying to keep his expression cool, he passed the envelope to her. "Here."

"Thanks," she mumbled. She stood tall and snapped her purse shut.

"Care to explain yourself?" he asked her.

Lorraine tucked her purse and the envelope under her arm. "Hunter, I swear, I had no clue who your father was."

"You expect me to believe it was a coincidence that you slept with me after befriending my father? You knew who I was when you saw me in the bar, didn't you?"

"No, I didn't."

He snorted in derision.

"I get it. This is the wackiest coincidence ever, so it's hard to believe we met by chance. But I'm telling you the truth. I had no clue. My God, if I *had*, I wouldn't have—" She stopped abruptly, not finishing her statement.

"Wouldn't have what?" Hunter asked, his eyebrows shooting up. "Spent the night in my bed?"

Lorraine's eyes frantically volleyed around at the passersby. She was worried that someone had overheard his comment. "Please," she whispered. "Don't do this."

There was a hitch in her voice, and he felt a tug inside his body. He wanted to be mad at her, but as he looked into her widened eyes, he was transported back to Friday night. The beautiful woman he'd held in his arms, her eyes filled with heat, not fear. The feel of her body trembling with desire beneath his. The way she'd dug her fingers into his skin and moaned into his ear...

Hunter's member began to harden, and it was like a jolt to the system. He was on the street, in broad daylight, and he was supposed to be angry. Not thinking about how amazing that night had been. What the heck was wrong with him?

Lorraine started to walk again, and that broke the spell. Hunter fell into step beside her. "Why'd you give me a fake name?"

Her jaw flinched. "I never expected to see you again," she said. "What did it matter if my name was Lorraine or Mary or Suzie Q?"

"It shows a deceptive side," Hunter pressed on, though he knew he was grasping at straws. She had given him a false name because she'd never planned to see him again. That reality stung his ego. No woman had ever ditched him before.

Plus he was trying to make sense of all that had happened. The incredible sex with her, then the disappointment of her leaving, and now learning that his father had left her in his will.

Her back stiffened. He saw a flash of anger in those beautiful brown eyes. "Deceptive how?"

"I think you got close to a vulnerable, dying man and encouraged him to leave you in his will."

"Yeah, I picked up on your seething distrust in the lawyer's office."

"What'd you expect me to do? Bring out the balloons? My father was not the kind of man who gave gifts to his own family. Why would he lavish gifts on a person he barely knew?"

"I've had enough of this," Lorraine announced, and walked the short distance to a silver Ford Fusion.

He followed her to the car and pressed his body against the driver's side door so that she couldn't enter. "Answer my question."

"I don't owe you any explanation," Lorraine shot back. Gone was the fear, replaced by irritation. "Get out of my way."

Hunter didn't move. Instead, he crossed his arms over his chest. "Answer my question," he repeated.

Lorraine looked beyond him to the passersby on the street. Then he saw the rise and fall of her chest as she inhaled deeply. "What question? All I'm hearing from you are accusations."

"In my shoes you wouldn't be suspicious?" he asked.

"I might be suspicious, but I wouldn't stubbornly ignore your explanation."

"What explanation? I'm still waiting for one."

Lorraine exhaled sharply, sounding exasperated. "I knew your father. The lawyer already made everything clear, didn't he? I was his palliative care nurse. I was there for him, and I guess he appreciated that."

"And he left you a store?"

Those beautiful lips parted, but it took her a moment to talk. "Perhaps if you'd been on speaking terms with your father, none of this would have come as a surprise."

Hunter flinched, as though she'd kicked him. Such lethal words from such pretty lips.

"You—me—*us*—that was totally a coincidence," she went on. "Think about it logically. Why would I have targeted you? To have to deal with this day, this moment? To deal with your suspicion and your wrath? Oh, yeah, great plan."

Hunter bit the inside of his lip. She made a good point. An excellent one, actually. But he wasn't about to concede. How could this be coincidence?

And in a flash, it came to him. Exactly why she might

have sought him out after manipulating his father. "It *was* a great plan," Hunter said. When her eyes widened, he went on. "A perfectly crafted one. You knew what you'd done with my father. Convinced him to leave you in his will. You probably thought that a man who never had any visitors would leave everything to you. Then you learned he didn't plan to cut his family out of his fortune, and you knew that you being a beneficiary likely wouldn't go over well with his rightful heirs. You probably asked him who his family was, did a little research. That led you to me. And then you targeted me, hoping that a night of sex would soften me when the ultimate blow of reality came today."

"Are you actually being serious?" Lorraine guffawed.

"I'm right, aren't I?"

"I'm not even going to dignify your ridiculous theory with a response," she said, squaring her chin defiantly. "Clearly, I made a colossal mistake at the bar by even talking to you. Biggest regret of my life."

Hunter's jaw flinched. Though that had been his exact thought when he'd seen her show up in Joseph Finkel's office, hearing her throw those words at him was like a slap in the face.

The truth was, he'd loved their night together. He'd thought about her constantly in the days that followed. He'd even returned to the bar on Saturday night, hoping to see her, figuring they could rekindle what they'd started. The night together had been that good.

"And so you know," she went on, "I don't plan to accept your father's gift. I never wanted anything from him. I'll call the lawyer later, tell him to have paperwork prepared to sign the store over to you. Will you now please leave me alone?"

Hunter's heart began to pound. Was she so desperate to be rid of him? "That's it? You never want to speak to me again?"

"What, after this pleasant conversation? Are you kidding me?" Lorraine ground out a frustrated breath. "I don't have time to deal with this. I'm getting a stress headache."

"All right. Then let's exchange numbers. We'll talk about this later."

Exasperation flashed in Lorraine's eyes. "Why? So you can continue to berate me?"

"You think my questions are *berating* you? My father did something I don't understand, and I'm not allowed to ask you about it?"

"You think you're the only one with questions?" Lorraine shot back, giving him a pointed look. "Where were you, by the way? Your father was dying, and he had no one. It broke my heart to see him like that, knowing that he was alone in this world. And yet he was a father. He had a son—you. But you weren't there for him when he needed you the most. In fact, you were so torn up over his death that you were out at a bar picking up strangers!"

Lorraine's words hit him like a knife to the chest, cutting deeper than before. He moved away from her car door and sucked in air, the pain inside him squeezing his lungs. The reality that he'd come home to find his father at death's door, and then for him to die so quickly, had left Hunter reeling from unexpected grief. It had suddenly become clear to him that their squabbles and disagreements didn't matter when it came to the big picture. And the big picture was that they were all each other had left of their family, and they should have been there for each other.

What made that reality harder to deal with was the fact that Hunter knew his father had wanted them to reconcile. Hunter was the one who had pushed him away. And he wasn't sure he'd be able to forgive himself.

But he said to Lorraine, "You don't understand."

"No. I don't understand," she agreed. "If that had been my father, I would have been there. Come hell or high water, no matter what grievances we'd had in the past, I would not let him die alone."

You think that's what I wanted? were the words that popped into Hunter's head. He hadn't even known his father was sick. But saying that to Lorraine wouldn't help the situation. His words would seem like a pathetic excuse.

"I'll talk to the lawyer," she said, pulling him from his thoughts. "Find out the steps that need to be taken to sign the property over to you. I'll see if we can get an appointment on Friday to get this over and done with. Clear your schedule."

Hunter's eyes narrowed in confusion. And before he knew what was happening, she was behind the wheel of her car. She started it, then drove away without giving him a second look.

Chapter 8

Lorraine pressed her foot down on to the gas pedal, accelerating at extreme speed. Her heart pounded wildly as she drove away.

She glanced in the rearview mirror. Hunter was still standing in the road where she'd left him. Still looking in her direction. Even from here, she could see the crestfallen expression on his face.

Lorraine turned right onto Blossom Street, her tires squealing as she did. Finally, Hunter was gone.

Only then did she loosen her fingers on the steering wheel, but she couldn't truly relax. If only the physical distance she was putting between her and Hunter could be permanent. But would she have to see him again in order to deal with the property Douglas had left her?

Of all the insane coincidences! Why did he have to be Douglas's son? Her stomach had bottomed out when he'd turned and faced her. She'd left his bed, never planning to see him again, only to have to face him across the table at the lawyer's office!

"This is what you get," she told herself. "It's your punishment for having a one-night stand."

Sleeping with a stranger had been totally out of character for her, and now she had lived to regret it.

Lorraine slowed down considerably and drove the rest of the way home at the speed limit. No point in getting a ticket on top of everything else today.

Her townhouse complex looked the same as it had

when she'd left. The beige stucco walls and orange clay roof hadn't changed. The palm trees were still stunning. It didn't seem possible that the rest of the world hadn't changed considering Lorraine's personal world had shattered.

Minutes later, she went into her end unit and collapsed onto her bed, where she stayed for over an hour. She forced in easy breaths, trying to get herself to relax, hoping she would fall asleep. But she couldn't put the day's events out of her mind.

After an hour of reliving the morning's horror and getting no rest, Lorraine threw off the covers and sat up. Her stomach roiled, but she knew it wasn't because she hadn't eaten solid food yet. She was sick over the shock she'd received this morning.

A prickly sensation raced down Lorraine's arms and back. She needed something to calm her nerves, but she wasn't sure anything *could* make her feel better. The way Hunter had glared at her...

Lorraine trudged out of her bedroom and went to the kitchen, where she set the kettle to boil. Perhaps some lemon balm tea would do her some good right now. And she really ought to eat something.

Maybe some oatmeal with bananas and walnuts. She frowned. No, she wanted something more convenient. She wanted comfort food.

Her eyes went upward to where she kept her guilty pleasure. A bag of plain salted potato chips was unopened on top of the fridge. Lorraine quickly snatched it as though she were scooping up a hundred dollar bill. She tore open the bag, and the fragrant scent of the fried potatoes filled her nostrils. Lorraine inhaled a deep, satisfying breath.

Not bothering with tea, she went to the living room with the bag of chips and sank onto her sofa.

It was one thing for her to sleep with a man she'd never

expected to see again. But then to not only see him, but learn that he was her deceased patient's son? And then to suffer through his glares once the lawyer announced what his father had left her in his will?

Lorraine stuffed more chips into her mouth, but the salty flavor she loved didn't make her feel any better. It had been bad enough seeing Hunter this morning. But what absolutely devastated her was the fact that he thought she had used his father. That she'd preyed on him.

Lorraine had done no such thing. She had simply been kind to a man who'd needed someone. She hadn't spent time with him with the hopes of receiving anything. She'd done it only to put a smile on his face. And one of the reasons she'd had to take the leave from her job was because of him. She'd grown especially close to Douglas, almost as if he'd been her own father. Having lost her father to a heart attack when she'd been a child, Lorraine barely remembered him. For the first time in her life, she'd connected with Douglas the way she imagined she would have connected with her father. Though she hadn't known Douglas long, and despite the fact that he was dying, he'd asked about her hopes and dreams, given her encouragement to pursue her passion. He'd even asked her what she thought would be the ideal location for her store. It had never occurred to Lorraine what he was up to. She'd simply enjoyed talking to someone who actually cared about what she wanted to do with her life. Her own husband certainly hadn't.

Her relationship with Douglas had been mutually beneficial. Douglas had enjoyed her company, cherished their visits and had looked forward to seeing her each day. Lorraine had enjoyed spending time with him, and had especially loved their talks and his support of her dreams.

When Lorraine had been granted the leave of absence and told Douglas that she wouldn't be around for a while, he'd been heartbroken. She'd seen it in his eyes. She had promised to come and visit him, and it was a promise she'd planned to keep after she had a little time to rest and de-stress.

But only a week after Lorraine had taken her leave, she'd gotten word that Douglas didn't have much time left. He'd asked for her, and Tami, one of her colleagues, had called her. Told her to come quickly. Lorraine had gotten there just in time, and even as Douglas's life was slipping away, he'd smiled at her. There'd been relief in his eyes. He'd taken her hand and hoarsely said, "Thank you."

Lorraine put down the bag of potato chips and wiped tears from her eyes. For Hunter to even think that she'd done anything to take advantage of his father really hurt her. The truth was, she'd come to love the man. And she'd certainly been there for Douglas when no one else had.

More tears filled Lorraine's eyes. It suddenly hit her—really hit her—that Douglas had left her the gift of her dreams. His hoarse whisper of thanks in his final moments held more meaning now. He'd left her this gift because he appreciated her. And dare she say, as a gesture of love.

But not the kind of love Hunter had implied.

A bitter taste filled Lorraine's mouth, and she swallowed. Right now, she should be crying happy tears of gratitude and love. Despite her sadness, she should feel a sense of fondness remembering Douglas and realizing just how much he'd cherished their friendship. Instead, her insides were twisting painfully.

Lorraine went to the kitchen and prepared the cup of lemon balm tea. An image of Hunter, smiling at her in the bar, popped into her mind. The next instant, that flirty face morphed into an angry, suspicious one. She pressed her hands against the kitchen counter and tightly closed her eyes, trying to push thoughts of Hunter out of her mind.

But she could never forget the fury simmering in his eyes hours earlier.

Despite being touched by Douglas's gift, she would never be able to keep it knowing that Hunter thought the worst of her. For that reason, she would willingly sign over the store to him.

She sipped her lemon balm tea, and it burned her tongue. "Damn it," Lorraine cried out, fresh tears springing to her eyes. But she wasn't really crying about the tea. Her body was jittery, her insides twisting and her temples pounding. All sorts of sensations and emotions were raging inside her. Happiness. Sadness. Love. Grief.

Horror.

She would have appreciated it if Hunter had spoken to her calmly and rationally about the situation. Instead, he'd jumped to horrible conclusions. She'd shared her body with him without reservation, and not only had the sex been explosive, they'd connected on a deeper level. How many times had she whispered how much she'd liked what he was doing, and begged him to touch her here, there…? They'd been instantly comfortable in the bedroom— shouldn't he have given her the benefit of the doubt?

Their chemistry had been immediate and hot, their night together off the charts. They'd been playful in bed as well as passionate—something Lorraine hadn't expected. In fact, their easy connection was one of the reasons she'd slipped out of his bed once he'd fallen asleep. She'd just ended a marriage. The last thing she wanted to do was jump into a new relationship.

And something about how well they'd gotten along had told Lorraine that she could easily see herself wanting to spend more time with a guy like Hunter. If he kept thrilling her in the bedroom the way he had, how long before she fell for him? So she'd left, happy to have a sizzling memory of their amazing night together.

But Hunter's instant suspicion of her had rendered their night together meaningless.

Lorraine rubbed her temples. The throbbing in her head was turning into a dull ache. She needed to do something—anything—to keep her mind off this morning's events.

The great thing about her townhouse complex in Ocean City was the pool and fitness center. Keeping active was always something Lorraine did when she wanted to de-stress. It was a picture-perfect day, with temperatures already in the high seventies. A perfect day for a swim.

Lorraine donned her swimsuit and went to the pool. She loved this area of the city. It boasted a lot of townhouses surrounded by lush gardens, bright flowers and majestic palm trees. The pool was enclosed by a wrought-iron gate and had palm trees in each of the four corners. There were several lounge chairs, but today only two had towels on them. A woman and two small children frolicked in the splash pad.

The rectangular-shaped pool wasn't quite Olympic-sized, but it was definitely large enough for the serious swimmer to do some laps.

As Lorraine made her way to the far end of the pool deck, she wondered why more people didn't take advantage of the building's pool. Yes, people worked and didn't have time to lounge around all day. But a surprisingly few number of men and women took the time in the evening to relax. They were far too overworked and stressed out—two things that helped encourage disease in the body.

Manuel, one of the building's maintenance workers, paused from clearing debris around the base of one of the palm trees and waved at her from across the pool. Stopping at a lounge chair on the opposite side of the deep end, Lorraine waved at him. Manuel whistled when she began to take off her bathing suit cover.

She fluttered a dismissive hand, wishing that Manuel's

compliment would lift her mood as it had so often in the past. Instead, her chest tightened. She couldn't get Hunter from her mind.

Lorraine walked to the deepest end of the pool and dove right in. She swam a half-length under the surface, then came up for air, gasping. She switched to the breast-stroke, pushing herself hard until her limbs burned. She hit the far end of the pool, turned and swam back. Then again, and again.

With each stroke, with each muscle working harder and harder, she prayed the physical pain would take away the memory of the day's stress.

Four laps later and physically spent, Lorraine finally came up for air. She rested her arms on the edge of the pool deck at the deep end and gasped in several breaths.

Manuel wandered over to her. "You okay?" he asked.

"Uh-huh." Lorraine pushed the loose strands of hair from her eyes.

Manuel eyed her skeptically. "You're swimming like the devil is chasing you."

"I've had a bit of a stressful day," she told him, holding up a hand to protect her eyes from the sun as she stared up at him.

"Already? It's barely noon."

"Oh, yeah," Lorraine said, the memory of Hunter's scowling face jumping into her mind.

"If it has to do with your ex, you want me to deal with him?" Manuel asked, his tone playful.

It was something he had jokingly stated in the past when she'd shared the facts about how Paul had made her life hell. "Naw," Lorraine said. "Wouldn't want you to go to jail a few years shy of your retirement."

Manuel was in his early sixties, and one of the maintenance men who always had a kind word for all of the residents.

"Yeah," he said, "you're right. Maria would be upset if ruined the plan to return to Guatemala when we retire. Not to mention what my kids would think of me."

"See?" Lorraine said. "Not a good plan. Don't worry, can take care of myself."

"I just don't like seeing you unhappy," Manuel said. "That ex of yours always makes you so miserable."

Lorraine offered him a weak smile. Of course, today's stress had nothing to do with her ex. But Manuel didn't need to know that. And the last thing she wanted to do right now was get into the whole sordid deal regarding Hunter.

"I'm fine," Lorraine said. "Don't you get gray hair over me."

Manuel laughed and rubbed his bald head.

Lorraine chuckled. Then she pushed off the pool's edge and began to swim on her back, hoping that she could finally push thoughts of Hunter out of her mind.

Hours after the meeting with the lawyer, Hunter was standing on the deck in the backyard of his father's house, the same house he'd grown up in. The same house he'd avoided for years. He frowned as he stared out at the general state of disarray.

Weeds were thriving in the grass, the white paint was peeling from the deck's floor. The shingles on the shed's roof were visibly deteriorating.

How long had his father been ill? It wasn't like him to let a property get out of control to this degree. For years, his father had flipped houses—something he'd taken pride in. He'd enjoyed taking houses that were in horrible conditions and turning them into beautiful homes. Yet he'd let his own home fall apart?

Hunter's throat thickened as he continued to look around. He drew in a slow, even breath, trying to shake the wave of emotion that hit him. Was it possible that his father had let this property run into the ground because without any family here, he didn't see it as a home?

Hunter understood the feeling. After the death of his twin sister, there'd been a void in this house. Neither of his parents had been the same jovial people they'd been before Ava's tragic passing. The strain on their relationship had been obvious to him, even though he'd only been twelve at the time. Before, Hunter's parents had enjoyed taking walks and holding hands, snuggling on the sofa and watching a movie, and going out for date nights. All four of them enjoyed Sunday night charades, going out to play tennis at a local court, and spontaneous road trips in the summer. Their house had been a fun and loving home.

And then they'd lost Ava. And the glue that held the family together had crumbled. It had been devastating enough to lose his twin sister, but he'd lost his mother, too, because a piece of her had died along with Ava. Four years later, she'd passed away for real, and Hunter would always believe that a broken heart had killed her. After his mother's death, the remnants of the relationship between Hunter and his father had disintegrated. Douglas had shut down emotionally as a father, while almost immediately getting involved with another woman. The relationship with a real estate agent had brewed so fast that Hunter couldn't help wondering if his father had been involved with Joanne before his mother's death. Two months later, Douglas and Joanne were married.

Even if his father hadn't been emotionally aloof before his involvement with Joanne, the marriage had signified an end of Hunter's relationship with him.

Hunter walked forward and gripped the deck's railing. A sliver of broken wood pricked his finger, stinging him the way the memory of that time in his life did. His father had put all of his attention into Joanne, while practically orgetting that Hunter existed. A vicious cycle had ensued, with Hunter acting out in a bid for attention from his father, and his father pulling away more and more because he didn't know how to deal with a difficult child. Hunter had been testing his father's love the way teens were apt to do, and his father's response had proven to him that he wasn't a priority in his life.

Douglas's marriage fell apart a year later, and he quickly moved on to the next woman. And the next. And Hunter's resentment had grown. The family home had become more like a prison, one he couldn't wait to break free from.

Finally, as an eighteen-year-old, Hunter had been able to forge out on his own. Nevada offered him the escape he desperately needed, while joining the fire service had allowed him to do something in honor of his sister.

Even as the years passed, the sudden loss of his twin had been hard to actually believe. To this day, Hunter couldn't accept what had happened. How could he accept the tragedy when "what if" questions had plagued him?

What if he hadn't been mad at Ava and she hadn't gone to a friend's house for the night?

What if his father and mother hadn't wanted a date night? Would Ava have bothered to go to her friend's house if she and Hunter hadn't been fighting?

What if Ava's friend's father hadn't been smoking?

What if, what if, what if… Those what if questions haunted a person.

Hunter had finally gotten a measure of peace when he'd thrown himself into his job, something that gave him purpose, even if he would never have true closure. Helping people and saving lives had been a saving grace for him.

He'd never expected to return to Ocean City, but the call he'd received from the hospice had changed everything. He'd learned that his father was dying and didn't

have much time left. Hunter knew then that he needed t
return home.

Hunter looked out at the unkempt lawn, and a wave o
regret washed over him. Suddenly, the weeds and brow
patches seemed like a metaphor for his messy relation
ship with his father.

His father had left him this house in the will, some
thing Hunter had expected but didn't want. Until today
he'd figured he would simply fix it up and sell it. But as
memories from the past flooded him, mixed with regret,
he wondered if he should consider living here.

His father hadn't been all bad. The fact that he'd im
pressed Lorraine said he'd done something right. Had he
simply been a dying man who'd changed his ways? Or
did Hunter not know his father as well as he'd believed?

Hunter went back into the house and took a seat on the
leather armchair, the same chair his father had liked to
occupy. It felt weird looking around the room from this
vantage point. He tried, for the first time, to put himself
in his father's shoes.

All these years, Hunter had blamed his dad for the disin
tegration of their bond. And, yes, his father certainly held
his share of blame. He'd pushed Hunter away when he'd
gotten involved with Joanne, putting the last nail in the
proverbial coffin on their relationship. Sure, they'd spo
ken over the years, but always briefly, superficially and
rarely. But over the last six months, his father had called
and emailed him more often. Hunter had ignored his fa
ther, keeping him at bay. And why?

Because he sensed that his father was trying to make
amends, and Hunter hadn't wanted any part of it. Never
once had his father apologized for emotionally abandon
ing him. So how could they suddenly become bosom bud
dies? Hunter had kept his father at arm's length, sending
him the occasional brief email stating that he was busy,

that he'd be in touch later. But he'd been waiting for an apology, because until then he wouldn't be able to even consider moving forward.

And now here he was, sitting in his father's chair, a feeling of heaviness bearing down on his chest. Seeing his father in the hospice, thin and frail and a far cry from the strong man he'd once been, had shaken Hunter to the core. At that moment, he realized how much he'd always hoped that some day they'd be able to get over the past. Now *some day* would never come.

"This is not your fault," he said aloud, the words reverberating in the room. This was his father's fault, the one who'd been an adult. Hunter had been young, and had needed his dad after the double blow of losing his sister and mother. Instead, his father had left him alone to navigate the ocean of grief as a teenager. It was hard enough for any person to deal with the premature loss of two family members, let alone a child.

The heaviness in his chest grew worse, like a weight pressing down on him. He could hardly draw in air. This house was filled with memories he'd tried so hard to bury, because they were too painful. He and Ava fighting over the last chocolate chip cookie their mother had made. Him licking the spoon of the cake batter after his mother had whipped up a batch of her delicious lemon cake. The family gathered in the living room to watch a Saturday night movie and eat popcorn. They'd had some happy times. The memories had been buried so deeply, but being here again, they were coming to the surface.

The sound of his mother's laugh, warm and infectious, seemed to float in the room. Hunter smiled. And then a wave of sadness gripped him. Not just for him and what he'd lost, but also for what his father had lost. His parents had been high school sweethearts, inseparable. He must

have been in a world of pain after losing the woman who
been the love of his life.

"I shouldn't have shut you out, Dad," Hunter said aloud
"If only I'd known you were sick. I'm so sorry."

But sorry now was too little, too late, wasn't it? Becaus
his father couldn't hear him. Hunter should have spoke
to his father while he'd been alive.

Despite their troubled relationship, Hunter had love
his father. Did his father know that? Before he'd passed
had he known?

Lorraine. Her name popped into Hunter's mind. She'
spent a lot of time with his father. They'd gotten extremely
close. Had his father spoken to her about their relationship

It was highly likely that he had.

Hunter needed to know what he'd said. Lorraine wa
the only one who had the answers he desired.

He needed to talk to her. As soon as possible.

Chapter 9

Lorraine waited until nearly the end of the work day to text Rosa. She needed to talk to her friend about what had happened this morning, and it would have to be an in-depth conversation. Probably over a good meal and a glass of wine. A recap over the phone simply wouldn't do.

At 4:30, Lorraine sent a simple text.

Dinner tonight after work? I need to chat.

Her phone rang shortly afterward. She answered Rosa's call after the first ring. "Hey, Rosa."

"What's going on?"

"Are you free to get a bite?" Lorraine asked.

"Well, I don't have a hot date. So I guess you're in luck."

Lorraine smiled. She could always count on Rosa to inject humor into a conversation. "I can meet you at five. Ruby's Café?"

"Sure. But what's going on? Everything okay?"

Lorraine sighed. "I'll tell you when I see you."

"Now you have me worried."

"I'll fill you in later," Lorraine told her. "See you soon, okay?"

Fifteen minutes later, Lorraine was out of the house and on her way to the café. When she arrived, Rosa was already there, sitting at a table facing the door. Rosa beamed and waved at her.

"I see my friend," Lorraine said when the hostess greeted her and offered her a menu.

Rosa got to her feet and opened her arms wide. Lorraine walked into her embrace. "Hey, girl!"

"Thanks for meeting me, Rosa."

Rosa waved a dismissive hand when she pulled apart from Lorraine. "Of course." She raised an eyebrow. "As long as you're buying."

"Ha!" Lorraine took a seat at the table. "That's the price of this girl talk, is it? Definitely cheaper than therapy, so I won't complain."

Rosa took a seat opposite Lorraine. Her expression turned to serious. "What's going on?"

Lorraine rubbed her temples, then folded her arms on the table. "Remember I told you I was going to the lawyer's office today?"

Rosa frowned. "It didn't go well? I figured you'd be happy after the meeting…?"

"*Happy* is the last word I'd use to describe how I felt this morning." Lorraine blew out a frazzled breath. "You won't believe what happened."

The waitress arrived at the table with two glasses of white wine. "There you are," she said. "Do you need more time to check out the menu?"

"Yes, please," Lorraine told her.

When the waitress walked away, Rosa said, "I took the liberty of ordering us wine. Riesling, your favorite. I had a feeling we'd need it."

"Good call," Lorraine told her. She lifted her wine glass and took a sip.

"Don't keep me in suspense," Rosa pleaded. "What happened at the lawyer's office? The family gave you a hard time?"

"Remember the guy at the bar?"

"Mr. Hottie? How could I forget him? The one you were

so into that you sprinted out of the b—" Rosa's words died in her throat, and were followed by a gasp. "Oh, my God. *You're not saying—*"

"He was there," Lorraine said. "In the lawyer's office."

"He was the lawyer?" Rosa surmised, her eyes growing as wide as saucers.

"Worse," Lorraine told her. And when Rosa's eyes narrowed, Lorraine explained. "He's the *son*. The son of the man who died."

"No!" Rosa exclaimed. Then in a not-so-hushed voice, "You slept with your patient's son?"

Lorraine quickly glanced left and right, hoping that no one within earshot had heard Rosa. She edged across the table and began speaking in a lower voice. "Honestly, I have to be *the* unluckiest person in the world. It's like the universe is punishing me for having a one-night stand."

"Or, forcing you back together," Rosa said, her voice rising on a hopeful note. "You did say you had an amazing night with him."

"That's *definitely* not going to be happening," Lorraine said. She snorted. "God, Rosa. It was awful. For a moment, I was so stunned. I thought I was imagining things. I mean, how could he be there? And the look on his face—he was as shocked as I was. But if only it was just shock."

"What do you mean?"

"He didn't see the situation as it was—a bizarre coincidence. He thought…" Lorraine paused, swallowed. "He thought I targeted him that night in the bar. He thinks I used his father in order to be left in the will."

"What?"

"I know, right? It's absurd. But the look he gave me… I swear. It was filled with hate."

"Did you guys have some big confrontation in the lawyer's office?"

Lorraine sipped more wine. "No. We didn't let on that

we knew each other. But Hunter followed me out when I left the office. He accosted me on the street."

"Oh, my God. He was that angry?"

"Yes. He thought the worst of me, and it made me feel like a pile of crap."

"But why?" Rosa asked. "You had such a great night together."

"It didn't help that I gave him a fake name. It made him all the more suspicious."

"Wait." Rosa frowned. "You gave him a false name?"

"I told him my name was Mary." When Rosa's eyebrows shot up, Lorraine continued, "I never expected to see him again. It was no big deal. I've never had a one-night stand before. Don't people lie about their names? Trust me, I was shocked to learn that Hunter's name was actually Hunter."

Rosa quickly sipped some wine. "I can hardly digest this. You slept with your patient's son."

"Can you please stop saying that?"

"It's just one of those crazy coincidences," Rosa said. "As soon as he realizes that, he'll calm down. It really doesn't make sense that you would target him."

The waitress arrived, and Lorraine ordered a salad, while Rosa ordered tacos. "We'll probably want more wine later," Rosa told the waitress.

Lorraine finished off her glass. "I'll take another glass right now." When the waitress walked off, Lorraine said, "So much for eating clean. But I need one more."

"You said Hunter followed you out of the office? How did it all end?"

Lorraine filled Rosa in on the conversation she'd had with Hunter on the street. "Only when I turned the tables on him did he back off. I asked him where he was when his father was dying, and pointed out that I'd never let my father die alone."

"Wow. That's serious drama."

"Tell me about it."

"You haven't even told me what's really important. You were left in the will. What was the gift?"

"Oh, that's right." Lorraine had been so consumed with the drama of seeing Hunter again that she wasn't even thinking about what Douglas had left her. "He left me a store. Said he wants me to open the health-food store that I've always wanted to. Can you believe it?"

Rosa's lips parted. "What?"

"I know. Incredible, right? I knew we formed a bond, but the last thing I expected was that he'd leave me in his will. Sometimes people will leave small monetary gifts for hospice workers. I wasn't aware that Douglas had any serious money, and I certainly didn't think he'd leave me anything even if he did."

"Your dream," Rosa said, her eyes lighting up. "You can finally make it a reality."

A lump formed in Lorraine's throat. She swallowed. "I can't accept it. Especially not with Hunter being so suspicious and angry."

"Whoa, wait a second," Rosa said. "I don't know about that. Think about it. You formed a real bond with your patient. You told me more than once that he was like a father to you. Maybe he thought the same about you, that you were like a daughter. If he wanted you to have the store, isn't it disrespectful to reject the gift he left you? Think about it. His gift will allow you to—"

"I know exactly what this gift will do," Lorraine interjected. And that was what hurt most of all. She would put the gift to good use. It was meaningful, and she would be able to help other people with it. But how could she accept it under such circumstances?

"No way should you give it up," Rosa went on. "If Hunter doesn't believe you, that's his problem. And like you asked, where was he when his father was dying, any-way? Did he actually answer you?"

"Not really." Lorraine had always fantasized about ask-ing Douglas's family members that question—where they'd been when Douglas was dying. Of course, she hadn't ex-pected that she would actually get that opportunity. But seeing Hunter in the lawyer's office, and being subject to his wrath, she'd been presented the opportunity.

"He may think you used his father, but at least you were there for the man. *He* left his father to die alone. How dare he question your motives, or his father's?"

"I totally agree." Lorraine snorted in derision. "Hunter should be ashamed of himself. Attacking my integrity?"

"Exactly," Rosa concurred. "And his father left you something because he wanted to. I hate how family mem-bers expect to get property and money simply because they're blood relatives. What, people aren't allowed to leave gifts to whomever they want? Girl, do not let him guilt you into giving up that store. How long have you talked about opening up a health-food store and clinic in honor of your mother?"

The waitress delivered their meals and Lorraine's sec-ond glass of wine. As Lorraine promptly took a sip, she pondered Rosa's words. She wished she had the same sen-timent as her friend. Yes, she'd love to see her dream come true sooner rather than later, but she had her pride to con-sider and she wasn't about to sell it out for anyone. She would prefer to return the gift and let Hunter do with it what he saw fit, rather than live under the suspicion that she had somehow manipulated a dying man into giving it to her.

Rosa picked up a taco smothered with cheese, tomatoes and jalapeños and took a bite. Lorraine stared at Rosa's plate, wondering if she should have indulged in comfort food instead of a salad. Not that a taste sensation in her mouth would make her feel better.

"No wonder you wanted to meet today," Rosa said. "Have you talked to Amanda and Trina about this?"

"Not yet," Lorraine said. She was closer to Rosa and shared her issues with her first. And as much as she wanted to get this off her chest with *someone*, she wasn't ready to tell Amanda and Trina about how the memory of her hottest sexual experience had been tainted.

Lorraine spiked a cherry tomato with her fork. As she brought it to her mouth, her stomach roiled. How could Hunter believe that she'd used her sexual wiles, or some other type of persuasion, to manipulate his father?

She sank her teeth into the tomato and chewed, but the flavors didn't register. Not when the only thing she could taste was the sour memory of what had happened.

The sexiest guy she'd ever slept with had turned into the biggest regret of her life. How could she ever get over that?

Chapter 10

On Thursday afternoon, when Hunter saw Joseph Finkel's number flashing on his cell phone, he quickly answered the call. "Joe," he said without preamble. "What's the news?"

"Well, I heard from Lorraine. She's decided she won't accept your father's gift. I explained that I'll have to draft a document that she'll need to sign, since the store is already hers. You'll also need to sign the paperwork. She can make it in tomorrow morning at ten. Can you come in that time, as well?"

"Wait." Hunter rose from the sofa in his condo, his heart pounding hard. "She's giving up the store?"

"She said that she doesn't want there to be any suspicion hanging over her head. She feels awful that this gift may be construed as something she pressured your father for." Joe paused. "What did you say to her when you left my office?"

Hunter swallowed, a spasm of guilt tightening his chest. "I—I wanted to find out how close she was to my father."

"That's all?"

"Yes," Hunter lied, because Joe didn't need to know that he'd slept with Lorraine.

"Perhaps your questions weren't well received," he said, and Hunter could hear the slight disapproval in the lawyer's voice. "In any case, I tried to assure her that no one suspected her of any wrongdoing, that your father was of sound mind when he added her to the will. I do understand her hesitation, however, especially when you talked to her against my advice." He paused again briefly, as if to make sure Hunter knew he wasn't pleased with how he'd handled the situation. "With that said," Joe went on, "perhaps you can assure her that you're okay with the will as is. Your father was quite adamant that he leave her a significant gift in appreciation of her care and friendship."

Hunter's gut twisted, conflicted emotions pulling at him. On one hand, he was glad that she was willing to denounce the gift. It meant she hadn't befriended his father for any sort of financial gain. But with that clarity came the guilt. She'd been there for his father, and his father had wanted to reward her for that. Now, because of him, Lorraine was going to give up the store that had been bequeathed to her. No argument, no fuss.

Hunter dragged a hand over his face and emitted a soft groan. Why had he been so hard on her? He shouldn't have questioned her motives. She wasn't the manipulative person he'd made her out to be.

His eyelids fluttered shut. He knew why he'd been so hard on her. Because seeing her in the lawyer's office— after last seeing her naked in his bed—had felt like some sort of betrayal.

"When do you want me to talk to her?" Hunter asked.

"Tomorrow at the meeting. I can be there, or if you'd like a moment alone with her, I'm fine with that, too."

"Perhaps a moment alone," Hunter said. Because what he needed to say to Lorraine was for her ears only. He'd been harsh, leveling accusations that had come from a place of confusion and hurt. The very thought that she'd deceived him, after how they'd torn up the sheets with some serious passion, had stung his ego. His immediate reaction had been to be a jerk.

Now that he had the perspective that came with time, he knew that the two of them getting together in the bar had nothing to do with his father. If it did, that would make her some sort of sociopath. Able to play her father, then play him. Maybe it was his own ego, but he simply couldn't accept the fact that she'd been faking their connection.

"All right," Joe said. "When she gets here, I'll leave you two alone."

"Thank you," Hunter said. "I look forward to the opportunity to make this right."

As he ended the call with the lawyer, he thought about Lorraine's parting words with him. *Where were you, by the way? Your father was dying, and he had no one. You weren't there for him when he needed you the most.*

Lorraine was right. He hadn't been there. He'd let his grievances with his father keep them apart. They'd been on such bad terms that his father hadn't told him about the extent of his illness until it was too late.

Lorraine's comment about him being out at a bar picking up women instead of mourning had cut deep. It wasn't that Hunter didn't care. It was that he'd been trying to escape his feelings of pain and guilt.

Obviously, he was in no position to complain about how his father spent his money or doled out his assets.

Tomorrow, he would make things right with Lorraine.

When Lorraine saw Hunter standing outside the lawyer's office building, she froze midstep. Her stomach tightened. What was he doing down here? He should be upstairs already, not here waiting for her. She'd specifically asked the lawyer to tell Hunter a meeting time of half an hour later than she was due to arrive because she wanted to make sure she didn't run into him.

Lorraine was arriving half an hour earlier than she was scheduled to meet with the lawyer, making it a solid hour before Hunter should be here. And yet there he was, standing outside the building's revolving door. He was wearing a short-sleeved cream-colored dress shirt, and with his hands on his hips his biceps were taut. His black tailored pants fit his muscular legs perfectly. Two women gave him an obvious head-to-toe look as they walked past him on to the street, then began to giggle. The women were heading in her direction now, and after sharing a whisper, they both glanced over their shoulders at Hunter.

"I wonder who he is," one of the women said.

"Let's go back and find out," her friend suggested.

Lorraine swallowed. Suddenly, she wanted to head over to Hunter. Make it clear that he was waiting for her.

Whoa, where was that thought coming from? Was she trying to stake her claim?

She stiffened her back and dismissed the ridiculous thought. She simply didn't want Hunter getting sidetracked by women hitting on him when he was here for an important meeting with her.

Lorraine turned, saw that the two women were continuing down the street, making her concern a nonissue. When she looked in Hunter's direction again, his eyes connected with hers.

Her stomach lurched. He lowered his hands from his hips and gave her a nod. Oh, God. Should she turn and leave?

One minute she'd wanted to go over to him, now she wanted to take off? Good grief, she was a big girl. She could handle seeing the man she'd slept with, even if it was uncomfortable. Humiliation never killed anybody.

It was just that she didn't want to have any conversations with Hunter outside of the lawyer's office. Their last interaction had been extremely unpleasant, and it was best if everything between her and Hunter was kept strictly about business. Not about their unfortunate one-night stand.

He continued to stare, and she stood where she was, as though they were both involved in a standoff. Then she took a deep breath and squared her shoulders. She was ready to turn over the keys to Hunter. She needed to sign the paperwork in the lawyer's office to make it legal. If she left now solely to avoid having to talk to him outside of the lawyer's office, she'd have to reschedule the meeting. And that would only be delaying the inevitable.

Hunter started toward her, and Lorraine's pulse began to pound. But she didn't turn and flee.

"You don't need to be afraid of me," Hunter said as he reached her.

Was that the vibe she was sending off? That she was afraid?

"I—I'm not afraid of you," she said. She was unhappy, yes. Anxious, yes. But not afraid. She didn't believe for a second that he would hurt her. In fact, part of her problem was that she couldn't forget how incredibly they'd connected that night before she'd known who he was.

"Good," he said. "You saw me, and you suddenly looked uncomfortable."

"I don't want another confrontation," she said, sounding harsher than she'd intended. "We should be talking upstairs with Joe. Our only dealings should be in his office."

Hunter's lips tightened, but he quickly offered her a smile, though it looked more pained than anything else. An uneasy sensation unfurled inside her.

Guilt, she realized. Her tone had been brusque, and she'd stung Hunter with her words. Which hadn't been her intention.

"I don't want another confrontation, either," he said. "I'm sorry about that, by the way. I was wrong for how I handled things with you the other day."

She shifted from one foot to the next. "We should head upstairs."

"The whole reason I'm down here is because I wanted to catch you before you went upstairs."

"I see," she said. Then, "Apology accepted." She made

a move to walk. But Hunter blocked her path. "What are you doing?"

"I haven't been waiting out here an hour just so you can go upstairs and avoid talking to me first."

"An *hour*?" He was that desperate to talk to her alone?

"As I said, I regret what happened the other day. I didn't react...maturely."

"Hunter, I would much prefer that we go upstairs and talk about this."

"I had a knee-jerk reaction," Hunter pressed on. "Imagine how I felt. One minute you were in my bed, then you disappeared on me. The next you're in my lawyer's office, where I learn that my father left you some property. It all seemed too coincidental. Too convenient."

"We've been through this."

"I know." Hunter blew out a breath. "I just want you to understand what was going through my mind when I saw you."

"How was I to know who you were?" Lorraine asked. "If I had, I sure wouldn't have spent—"

"You wouldn't have spent the night with me?" Hunter supplied when she stopped short of finishing her statement. "I know. You made that clear the other day."

"Would you have wanted to spend the night with me?" Lorraine challenged. "The fact that we happened to have a one-night stand has certainly complicated things, wouldn't you agree?"

Hunter's lips parted, but he didn't say anything. She took his silence for agreement. "Exactly," she said. "It would have been way too awkward."

"If you're asking me whether I regret our night together, I don't."

Lorraine inhaled sharply, a tingle of warmth spreading across her chest. She hadn't expected that response, and now she was the one who was speechless. Though it made no sense, a part of her was happy to hear that Hunter didn't regret their night. Because the truth was, she didn't regret that night, either.

Not that she was ever going to admit that, of course.

"After I went home," Hunter continued, "I thought about the situation. About you and me. About your connection to my father. And I realized that my knee-jerk reaction didn't make sense. Why would you single me out? But I was so shocked at the time that I didn't know how to process everything."

"But do you still think it's possible that I duped your father?"

Hunter hesitated, and Lorraine's heart sank. He *did*.

"Of course you do," Lorraine said, and started to walk.

Hunter fell into step beside her. "That's not what I'm saying. Lorraine, will you stop for a second?"

That tingle of warmth was turning into anger. Stopping, she placed her hands on her hips. "Perhaps if you'd been around for your father, you could have stopped me from taking advantage of him. I hope you've thought about that."

"I deserve that, I know." Hunter's shoulders slumped. "I'm trying to make things better, but I guess I'm making them worse. You must think I'm some sort of scumbag."

"Don't you think the same of me? What kind of woman would prey on a dying man?"

"Damn it, Lorraine. I'm not trying to fight with you. I want us to talk. Really talk. Maybe we can go to a café. There are plenty nearby."

"The lawyer's waiting on us."

"My dad and I... We had a rocky relationship. A lot of stuff happened in the past, stuff I'm not about to get into out here with people walking by every second. But suffice it to say, he never even told me he was sick. By the time I found out, I came here for him, and he was basically on his deathbed."

"Please, let's go up to the lawyer's office," Lorraine pleaded. She didn't like the vulnerable hitch she heard in Hunter's voice, the way he suddenly seemed far more human to her. She wanted to keep him purely in the enemy camp.

"Aren't you hearing me?" Hunter asked. "I don't want to go upstairs. Not before we talk. Besides, I already canceled the meeting, anyway."

"What?" Lorraine's eyes widened.

"I canceled the meeting."

Her jaw tightened, and she balled her hands into fists. "How could you?"

"Because your plan to sign the property over to me is a reflex reaction. You need to make that decision after you take a moment to really think about it."

"So now you *don't* want the store? You're infuriating."

"This was never about me taking the store from you. My dad left you that property for a reason. He got to know you, and obviously liked you and supported your vision. I don't want you to give it up because of me."

Lorraine stared at him, her heart thumping hard. What on earth was going on? "I don't understand."

"There are a dozen coffee shops within two blocks of here. Pick one you like. Let's sit down, have a reasonable conversation."

As if Lorraine wanted to do that! She didn't want to spend more time with him. She wanted to get this over with. Already her pulse was racing, and a myriad of sensations was rushing through her. The man was gorgeous, and that very fact was distracting her. She wanted to sign the papers and never see Hunter again.

She wanted to kiss him.

Whoa… *What?* Where had that thought come from?

"No," she said.

"No?" he asked, his brow furrowing.

"I don't want to talk to you anywhere but in Joe's office," she said.

"Are you always this hardheaded?" Hunter asked.

"You don't want to take no for an answer and you dare to call me hardheaded?"

Hunter crossed his brawny arms, and Lorraine instantly understood why she was so uncomfortable around him. There was tension between them. The kind of tension that manifested itself in an argument… Or in the bedroom.

She turned around and counted to three. She needed to get a hold of herself. She was stressed. That was normal. She'd slept with a stranger, and it had come back to haunt her. But life went on. "Look," she began, "I appreciate that you're coming around to understanding that I wasn't using your father. But I've made up my mind. The gift is too much. I can't accept it. Did you really cancel the appointment?"

"I did."

The nerve of the man! But she took a moment before speaking and deliberately kept her voice calm. "I'm sure Joe can still see us. I'll call him—"

"I'm not going to sign any papers until you agree to talk to me."

"So everything has to be on your terms?"

"It's a simple request."

Lorraine guffawed. Simple… Yeah, right. "This isn't about you. I've thought about this since we left the lawyer's office. Long and hard. And it just feels wrong for me to accept something like this from your father. He should have left whatever he had to his family. I don't want to stand in the way of that."

"What am I going to do with it?" Hunter asked. "Sell it and go on a luxury vacation?"

"If that's what you want, sure."

He placed his hands on his hips and turned away from her. His body language screamed frustration.

He wasn't the only one.

But frustration was good. The more annoyed he was with her, the more likely he'd agree to go upstairs and finalize their arrangement.

He faced her. "You want to open a health-food store? Some kind of clinic?"

"Yes," Lorraine said cautiously. "Why?"

"I want to hear about this shop. Why he left it to you."

"It's self-explanatory."

"Humor me. I want to understand my father better. You're the best person to help me understand him. You spent a lot of time with him. I want to know what about your vision appealed to him." Hunter paused. "Take me to the storefront. Let's go look at it together. We can talk there."

The man's face must have been plastered in the dictionary next to the word *stubborn*. "And if I say no?" Lorraine asked.

His expression was the only answer she needed.

"Hunter—"

"You want me to sign the paperwork," he said, holding her gaze. "This is the only way."

"Oh for goodness' sake." Lorraine blew out a huff of air. "Fine. If that's what it takes, I'll show it to you."

"We can take my car. It's right there." He pointed to a sleek navy blue BMW.

Oh, no. She wasn't about to get into a car with him. "I don't think so," Lorraine said. "You can follow me there. Because that's the only way I'm going anywhere with you."

"All right," Hunter said. "Deal."

Chapter 11

Ten minutes later, Lorraine was pulling up in front of the storefront Douglas had bequeathed her. She sat in her car for a long moment before getting out. Even though Rosa had encouraged her to check out the store, she hadn't been able to bring herself to do that. Knowing that she wasn't going to keep it had made the idea of checking it out all the harder. To see her dream so close, but yet so far… Why put herself through that? The most Lorraine had been able to do was drive by it once, simply to say she'd seen it.

Now knowing that she was actually going to enter the building had her stomach tensing.

She looked out at the street, with young families passing by casually. Some had ice cream cones, some walked dogs. The general vibe was warm and relaxed.

It truly was the perfect location. This section of Ocean City was like a village within a city, with mom-and-pop type businesses amidst low apartment complexes and townhouses. The trendy area got a lot of foot traffic. There was no other store like the one Lorraine envisioned nearby, and it would be the perfect place for her to set up a health-food store and nutrition clinic.

The sound of knuckles knocking against her window caused her to jump. Her heart nearly imploded in her chest. She glanced out at Hunter, then raised a finger to tell him that she needed a minute. After a moment, she turned off her car and opened the door.

Why was she even thinking about how perfect this location was? She wasn't going to keep it. She would do what she'd always planned—work for her dream. It would take a lot longer, but so be it.

She exited the car and stared out at the storefront, which had large windows that were covered by blankets from the inside. A father walked by with his young daughter sitting around his neck. A small dog wagged its tail and veered toward Lorraine, its tongue lolling.

"Oh, hello," Lorraine said, dropping onto her haunches to pet the friendly little guy. "Cute dog," she said to the father when he guided it back on its leash.

"She loves saying hi to everyone," the man explained.

They continued on, and Hunter sidled up beside her. "Seems like a nice neighborhood. A lot of foot traffic, and people seem friendly."

"Mmm-hmm," Lorraine agreed.

The very reason she hadn't wanted to go into the store was because she hadn't wanted to get attached to this location. Standing in front of it now caused a rush of emotions to wash over her. She was literally standing in front of her dream.

Slowly, Lorraine made her way toward the store, looking up at the blank spot where a name should be. Hunter walked with her. "So, this is it," he said, stating the obvious.

Lorraine nodded. "Yeah."

"What would you name it?"

Her eyes flew to his. "Is that really necessary?"

"Like I told you, I want to hear your vision. I want to hear why my dad was sold on you opening this place."

"I haven't really decided." Hunter cast her a sidelong glance, and Lorraine wasn't sure if he believed her. "I've had some ideas, but I really wanted to be inspired by the neighborhood. And since I'm not planning to keep this..." Her voice trailed off.

"Okay. Why don't we go inside?" Hunter suggested.

Lorraine didn't really want to go inside, especially not with Hunter, but what choice did she have? She withdrew the envelope, retrieved one of the two keys and unlocked the door.

Hunter quickly pulled the door open and held it for her. Lorraine crossed the threshold.

The breeze from outside stirred up the dust mites, causing them to swirl in the open space. A space that was larger than Lorraine ever could have hoped for. To the right, there was a large counter, covered in a tarp. The shelving was on the left and was covered by large white sheets. The room went back quite far, and actually extended to the right.

"It's a pretty decent size," Hunter said, looking around.

"Larger than I expected," Lorraine said.

"Tell me about your plans for this place."

"I already told you," Lorraine said, exasperated. "I'm not keeping—"

"Hypothetically," Hunter stressed. "What are your plans *hypothetically*?"

Slowly, Lorraine turned, taking in a 360-degree view of the space. Then she blew out a heavy breath. "Okay." She gestured to the left. "I imagine having health-food supplements on this wall here. It'd be perfect." She pointed to the far back right of the store, where she could see a door that led to a back room. "In the back section, I would have a clinic. A place where I could give people advice about nutrition and diet. I'd set up blood pressure testing as well, the do-it-yourself type that you find at pretty much every drugstore. Ideally, I would have a dietician working with me. I want to sell healthy supplements and natural remedies, but I really look forward to the opportunity to work one-on-one with customers who need nutritional advice to get their health back on track. As the saying goes, you are what you eat, and people eat so much junk, it's no wonder so many people are unwell."

"I agree," Hunter said. "Go on."

She turned, looking back toward the front door. "Besides nutritional supplements, it would be nice if I could have a part of the front of the store dedicated to fresh produce. We don't live in a food desert, but it'd be nice to support local farmers. Have them sell their fresh organic fruits and vegetables to provide an alternative to all the fast-food places around here. Oh, and if there's room, I'd have a section in the back where fresh juices and smoothies could be made with healthy ingredients."

"So you're a health nut."

"I'm not perfect, and I've certainly had too much wine lately." She smiled softly. "But I try to eat well at least eighty percent of the time." As a teen, she'd always craved junk food when upset, but as she got older she'd tried her best to curb those cravings by going for a swim or a run.

"What kind of health and nutrition advice?" Hunter asked.

"Oh, anything and everything, I guess. I really hate that as a nation we're overprescribed on drugs when natural remedies can solve a lot. For example, I've had personal experience with type 2 diabetes in my family, and I know it's a diet-related disease. A lot of people don't know that it can be reversed if you eat the right foods. It's not just about cutting down on sugar and poking yourself to see what your blood levels are. If you change your nutrient intake, you can do wonders for your body and reverse the disease."

Hunter's eyebrows rose. "Really?"

"Yep," Lorraine said. "Anyway, I would offer healthy eating plans and exercise tips. Maybe even some cooking classes. I know I'm going to have to start small, but if I could wave a magic wand, that's the big vision I'd like to make a reality. I'd love to have a place like that in the community that could dramatically change lives."

"Now I see why my father liked you."

Hunter smiled at her, and Lorraine's lips parted. Warmth filled her chest.

"I like that your vision is about giving back. It's noble."

Hunter's words were stoking the embers of desire on her dream. She had come here with the resolute decision to sign the store over to him, but talking about her greatest passion had her suddenly wanting the dream more.

"You really do enjoy helping people." It was a comment, not a question.

"My mother had type 2 diabetes and high blood pressure, and when she switched to a better diet, all of her problems went away. I saw firsthand that the power of nutrition was something real. I'm not saying everything can be cured or prevented with diet, but a lot can." Lorraine stopped abruptly. "Anyway, I don't mean to bore you. It's something I'm particularly passionate about." She smiled softly. "I wish I could snap my fingers and be ready to execute my plan today, but all the things I told you and everything I want to do will take years of planning. So as much as I'm grateful to your father for offering me this building, I can't accept it for a number of reasons."

Hunter took a step toward her, and Lorraine sucked in a breath. "I think there's only one reason why you don't want to accept it," he said. "Me."

Again, Lorraine's heart began to thump. There was something contrite in his eyes. And it endeared her to him.

"That's not true," she said. "I just told you that I'm not ready yet. I need to get my business plan together, all of that stuff."

"You just pitched me your business plan, and you sold me on it. My father, even though he was dying, saw the value in what you wanted to do. I'm sure he told you that."

Lorraine nodded. "He did."

"And now I understand why. And it makes me appreciate him even more. For much of my life I saw my father as selfish. He was dying. He could've easily cared only about his plight, and rightfully so. Instead, he wanted to do something that would help you help more people." Hunter glanced away, but Lorraine didn't miss the way his face contorted with emotion. "He wasn't as bad as I thought he was."

"The man I knew was really sweet. Whatever kept you two apart—"

"You have a sound plan," Hunter said, facing her. "I don't want to take that away from you."

"I've made up my mind," Lorraine said, determined to minimize her time with the tempting, infuriating man. "And it has nothing to do with you."

One of his eyebrows rose as he looked down at her. He didn't believe her.

"No, seriously," she said. But she was lying. The financial part of her dream—the biggest and most challenging part—indeed *had* been handed to her on a silver platter, and Lorraine didn't want to accept it. Because everything inside of her right now was telling her that she needed to make a clean break from Hunter and never look back.

He closed the distance between them, and looked down at her, holding her gaze. He raised his hand, then began to lower it again. Finally, he lifted it to her face and softly stroked her cheek.

Lorraine drew in a startled breath. His fingertips moved over her skin, gently, almost reverently. "Don't let the fact that I was a jerk change your plans," Hunter said softly. "Don't let anyone take your dreams away from you. Especially not some guy you met in a bar and had a one-night stand with."

Lorraine's heart was pounding so hard, she could hear

it thundering in her ears. Why was he touching her? An
why, right now, did he mention their night together? I
brought a flush of heat to her skin.

"I'm sorry," Hunter said, his voice a whisper, an
a shiver of desire raced down her spine. "I was just s
shocked to see you again after the way you left me. Mayb
that's what really had me upset—that you took off on me.
thought… I thought we both had fun." His fingertip movec
to the corner of her mouth. "Didn't we?"

Was he seriously asking her this? "I…" Lorraine
couldn't summon any words.

Hunter trailed his finger along her bottom lip, and desire pooled in her belly like hot lava. She wanted to take
his finger into her mouth and suckle it.

"Why *did* you leave me?"

He brought his other hand to her face and began to
stroke her skin, and Lorraine barely breathed. She stood
there like an inanimate object, unable to move. Hunter was
touching her. And just like when she'd first met him, she
couldn't tamp down on the intense reaction she had to this
gorgeous man. Tingles of pleasure were coursing along her
flesh and spreading to every corner of her body. Despite
telling herself that she never wanted to see Hunter again,
she knew in this moment that what she really wanted was
nothing more than to get naked with him again.

"Didn't you have as good a time as I did?" Hunter asked.

Lorraine's knees became like jelly, and she stumbled
backward. Hunter scooped a hand around her waist, but
she quickly shrugged out of his touch. "No," she said, her
senses coming to her. His fingers no longer on her skin,
his eyes no longer locked with hers, the spell between
them was broken.

"No?" Hunter asked.

Lorraine didn't look at him. She knew he'd miscon-
strued her response. "Not no, I didn't like it. I mean, no.

don't want you to touch me anymore. This is… What's our agenda?"

He took her by the shoulders and forced her to face him. 'Agenda? I'm trying to make things right between us."

"By…touching me? You're trying to charm me, but do you really expect me to melt in your arms?"

"Would that be so bad?"

"Oh, my God," Lorraine said, jerking her body backward awkwardly. She had to get away from him. "Is that what this was about? You talked a good game about wanting to hear my vision, but you really just wanted to get me alone again—didn't you? You wanted to seduce me again!"

"*I* seduced you, did I?" He gave her a pointed look. "I think we both seduced each other."

Lorraine's face flamed. The situation was unraveling. They were so off point, it was ridiculous. "You're right. I can't keep the store because of you. This, us, it's wrong, it's awkward. Do with the store what you like. I have to get out of here."

She started for the door.

"Did I just imagine our amazing connection?" Hunter asked. "Or are you running because you don't want to admit how much you enjoyed yourself in my bed?"

Lorraine halted at the door. Oh, how she wanted to turn around, throw him the keys and tell him to never talk to her again.

Liar, a voice sounded in her head. That was the last thing she wanted to do. Her body was flushed, her pulse racing. Lust for Hunter was coursing through her veins as though she'd been injected with a potent drug.

She sensed him behind her before she heard him. And when he slipped his arms around her waist and pulled her back against the hard wall of his chest, a long breath oozed out of her, her pent-up sexual frustration slowly being released.

"Tell me," Hunter whispered into her ear. A low groa rumbled in his chest as he smoothed his hands over he stomach. "Why do you keep running from me?"

"Hunter…" Lorraine lolled her head backward agains his shoulder. Good Lord, it felt so good to be in his arm again. "You said you wanted me to…to show you the store I don't understand what's…happening."

"There's something about you," Hunter said softly, in voice that was both unnerving and arousing. "Honestly, didn't come here to do this. I came here to understand my father's motivations a bit more. See you through his eyes But instead, all I can do is think about us and that night and the way you left me wanting so much more."

"This is crazy," Lorraine said, even as she leaned back against his body.

"If you're playing a game with me, just tell me. Because if you don't want this—" He stroked her cheek again, then let his fingers roam under her chin and down to the base of her neck. "I need to know."

His voice was soft and feathery, and Lorraine's eyes fluttered shut. She wanted to tell him to leave her alone. She wanted to give him the keys right now and run and never see him again. But not because she didn't want what he was offering. She wanted to run because she *did* want it.

He brushed his lips against her cheek. "Am I crazy?" he whispered into her ear. "Was what I felt with you in my bed one-sided?"

She swallowed. He'd asked the right question. Or rather, the wrong one. Because she couldn't answer him honestly now. She couldn't tell him that she *hadn't* enjoyed her time in his bed. So she said nothing.

"You don't like it when I touch you?" he asked, one of his hands moving up to cup her breast.

"You know I do," she rasped, finally telling him what he wanted to hear.

A satisfied groan emanated from his throat. He trailed his lips along her cheek. "I remember everything. Just how you like to be touched."

Lorraine's center pulsed. She was lost.

When the cell phone rang, her heart slammed against her rib cage. It sounded like an alarm going off in the room.

When it rang a second time, Hunter said, "Damn, that's mine. Hold on."

As he stepped away from her, coolness enveloped her. She blinked rapidly, her breathing haphazard. Though her brain knew that they'd just been interrupted by a phone call, her body didn't seem able to cope with the sudden desertion.

"No, this isn't a bad time," Hunter was saying when Lorraine turned to face him.

She placed a palm on her chest, surprised at how quickly it was rising and falling. What was wrong with her? A few heated words and a few gentle strokes and she'd been ready to get naked with him again?

The phone call had saved her from reacting with her libido, instead of thinking like a mature woman.

"I know," Hunter said. "We got delayed."

Lorraine's eyes narrowed. *We?* Who was he talking to?

"She's going to need another few days," he said.

Lorraine gaped at him. "Are you talking to Joe?" she asked.

Hunter held up a hand to keep her at bay. "Wait a minute, what letter?"

He'd lied to her, hadn't he? He'd told her that he'd canceled the appointment with the lawyer!

"Definitely, I'll come by and get it now," he said. "All right, see you soon."

When he ended the call, Lorraine shook her head. "Was that Joe?"

Hunter didn't meet her gaze. "Yes."

"You didn't really cancel the appointment, did you?"

"I did. But I promised to get back to Joe and let him
know what was happening. He said he could fit us in this
afternoon if we wanted to move forward with the paper
work."

"This afternoon? What time?"

Hunter's face fell. His disappointment was obvious. "I
was hoping you'd agree not to make a rash decision today.
To think the situation over, consider my offer."

"I'm happy to keep the appointment," Lorraine said. It
was the only way to escape Hunter and the power he had
over her. But when he closed his eyes and rubbed his tem-
ple, Lorraine knew in an instant that something was wrong.
"What is it?" she asked. "What's going on?"

Hunter opened his eyes and sighed. "Apparently, my
dad left me a letter. It's at Joe's office."

Lorraine frowned. "And he's just telling you about it
now?"

"He said my dad told him he didn't want me to get it
right after the will was read. He wanted Joe to give me
the letter a few days later, maybe a week. Joe said he was
planning to give it to me today. He's heading out of town
tomorrow, so he asked me to pick it up this afternoon."

"You look worried."

"I'm surprised." But the way his lips twisted told Lorraine he was more than surprised. He looked alarmed.

Perhaps a little afraid.

"You, um… You want me to—"

"I've got to go," Hunter said, cutting her off. Had he
even heard her speak?

Briskly, Hunter started for the door. "Hunter?" Lorraine said.

"I'll talk to you later," he said without breaking stride.

And then he whizzed out the door and was gone.

Chapter 12

Hunter ran along the waterfront, pushing himself to go harder and faster than he had before. His heart was pounding, his breathing shallow, and sweat was pouring down his face and bare torso. But he sprinted the last fifty yards to his condo building in the bike lane. He jumped the curb onto the sidewalk, then slowed and doubled over. He braced his hands on his knees and gulped in several deep breaths.

He raised his head, looked at the streaks of orange in the sky. The sun was setting, and the clear moon hung high. His mother had always loved sunsets, so whenever Hunter saw a spectacular one, he couldn't help thinking of her and feeling a sense of peace. But today, his stomach was twisting. No matter how far and fast he had run, he couldn't outrun the reality that the letter from his father was upstairs in his apartment, unopened.

"What are you afraid of?" he asked himself.

An older man who was walking by him looked in his direction. He must have thought Hunter was speaking to him. Hunter gave the man a brief nod, then headed toward the building's door.

Once he was upstairs, he went into the living room. He looked at the envelope, which he'd placed on the coffee table. His name was written in his father's familiar penmanship, though it was shakier than it used to be. How weak had his father been when he'd written this letter?

Hunter walked past the living room and into the kitchen,

where he opened the fridge and pulled out his pitcher of filtered water. He poured some into a tall glass, then downed it all in several gulps. He put the pitcher back into the fridge, then started toward his bathroom.

He stepped into the bathroom, then stopped and pivoted on his heel. Why was he delaying opening the letter?

He marched back to the living room, snatched up the envelope and opened it. He pulled out the single sheet of lined paper. A quick glance told him that his father had written on both sides.

He swallowed, then started to read.

Son,

I write this letter with a heavy heart.

I know I don't have much time left, and as I look back on my life, I'm filled with regret.

There's nothing more that I wanted than for you to be here with me, making up for lost time. But I understand why you're reluctant to talk to me.

My sincere hope is that when you read this letter, you and I will have spoken. I do not want to die without closure from you.

I know I was a horrible father. When we lost Ava, I didn't know how to cope. I blamed your mother because it was easy. And it tore her apart. It tore me apart. When our relationship soured, I put a wall around my heart. I suppose it was the only way for me to be able to deal with losing such a vital part of me. My little girl.

And then when we lost your mother, the pain was unbearable. I couldn't let it show. Not to you. I tried to be strong, but I was weak. I turned to someone else to make me forget. And in the process, I neglected you.

That wasn't my intention, and the worse things

got for us, the less I knew how to fix them. I take full responsibility for how our relationship fell apart. I don't blame you for leaving—you had nothing here. But even while you were gone, I loved you with all of my heart. Even if I couldn't express it. Even if I was too stupid to realize that your acting out meant you needed me even more.

Hunter, I hope that you've had some time to reflect on our relationship now that I'm gone. I hope we were able to talk first, because I know what regret feels like. When I lost your mother, part of the pain came from knowing that I had pushed her away. She'd died without us fully resolving our relationship and our love. And that broke me.

Please look back and remember me as the man I was before we lost Ava, and before we lost your mother. That's who I was without the pain. I became a different person because I was hurting so much. But I always loved you.

And I hope that when you think of me, it will be with love in your heart.

Sincerely,

Dad

PS—I've left a young woman named Lorraine a gift in my will. She was a godsend to me while I was sick. She's a nurse at the hospice, and in so many ways she was my angel. I'm sure you'll be surprised by my gift to her, but I hope you don't fight my wishes. Throughout my illness, Lorraine was my angel. In fact, she was like a daughter to me.

Hunter's stomach wrenched painfully, as if someone was pulling his insides in two different directions. He re-

read the letter, his throat constricting. He could hardly draw in breath.

These were the words he had wanted to hear from his father so desperately when he'd been young, and in the years that had followed when he'd fled to Nevada. He had simply wanted to know that his father still loved him.

And yet, his father hadn't been able to say any of this to him in person. Not years ago, and not even when Hunter had gone to visit him in the hospice the day before he'd died. Perhaps he'd been weak then, not able to say much. And maybe that conversation would have been too emotionally heavy when he didn't have much strength. Instead, his father had taken his hand. Hunter had seen the tears well in his eyes, and he'd choked back his own. The visit had been awkward, but welcome. For their short time together, physically connecting with his father had been enough.

And the next day, he'd passed.

While Hunter had been on his way back to Reno to testify in a criminal trial for which he had been a witness on the scene of the fire, his father had been taking his last breath.

Hunter folded the pages and stuffed them back into the envelope. Then he held the letter against his chest. His father had laid his heart out, finally giving Hunter the closure he'd always wanted. But not in the way he would have liked.

"Damn it, Dad. Why didn't you talk to me about this? Give me a chance to hash things out with you face-to-face?"

His head felt heavy, clouded with conflicting emotions. Sadness. Guilt. Regret. Because as much as Hunter wanted to blame his father for how badly things had gone, he knew he shared some of the blame, too.

And that reality rocked him to the core.

* * *

Lorraine scrolled the mouse down on her laptop screen, perusing the listings of businesses for sale and for rent in Ocean City. Each price she saw made her eyes widen and her heart sink. They were a lot higher than she expected.

The more reasonably priced places were about a half hour outside the city, but that wasn't where she wanted to have her business. At least not ideally. It would mean a daily commute, which wasn't what she desired.

Her eyes landed on an ad for a pleasant-looking storefront, with hanging pots of flowers on either side of the front windows. It looked pretty small, definitely smaller than the property Douglas had purchased for her. It was listed as a rental.

Lorraine lifted her phone. She was about to press in the number for the real estate agent, but hesitated. Months earlier, when she'd started casually checking out properties, an agent had advised her against a rental situation, because the landlord could change the lease terms at the end of the term. It had happened with a couple of money-hungry business owners who'd dramatically raised rental prices, leaving a few favorite dining places and boutiques out of business. Lorraine hated that kind of shamelessly selfish greed.

Lorraine's phone began to vibrate in her hand an instant before it started to ring, startling her. As she looked at the screen, she saw Rosa's smiling face. She quickly swiped to answer the call.

"Hey, Rosa," Lorraine said. "What's up?"

"I'm not sure. That's what I was hoping you could tell me."

Lorraine frowned. "What?"

"Did you see Hunter again yesterday? And I'm on my lunch break, so don't keep me waiting."

Lorraine's frown deepened. "How do you know that I saw Hunter?"

"Because he sent me a text. He asked me to tell you to call him because he needs to continue your conversation from yesterday."

"What are you talking about? How could he send you a text?"

"At first I was startled, too. Then I remembered that the night in the bar I wanted his phone number to make sure that if you went missing, I'd be able to go to the police with information." Rosa paused. "So…spill the beans!"

"We were supposed to meet at the lawyer's office yesterday so that we could sign the required paperwork for me to sign the store over to him."

"You're giving it up?"

"I was just about to call a real estate agent about another store when your call came through. It's a rental, but—"

"And how are you going to afford it?" Rosa challenged. "When you were looking for places months ago, they were all very expensive. Your divorce cost you a pretty penny. You've been left a gift by—"

"Look, I know." Lorraine blew out a frazzled breath. "I want to do it on my own, but you're right. It's going to be a huge challenge."

"And it's completely unnecessary. Stop being so stubborn. Oh, wait. I've got a call coming through."

Lorraine continued to peruse her laptop while she waited for Rosa to return to the line.

"Girl, Hunter really wants to reach you," Rosa said when she spoke again.

Lorraine's heart pounded hard. "That was him?"

"Yeah. He asked if I'd given you the message. I told him that I'm on the line with you now. He kind of sounds stressed."

The letter. When he'd left her yesterday, he'd looked

frazzled. Had he read something in the letter that hurt him? "He found out that his father had left him a letter. He seemed pretty upset. What's his number?"

Rosa recited the number for her. "Keep me posted."

"Talk to you later."

Lorraine immediately typed in Hunter's number. He answered after the first ring. "Hello?"

"Hunter, hi. It's Lorraine."

She heard a small exhalation of air. "Thank you for calling," he said.

"No problem. Are you okay?"

"I need to see you," he said. "It has to be today because I work tomorrow."

"Some time later this evening?" Lorraine suggested.

"Earlier would be better. I start my next twenty-four hour shift in the morning, so I'd like to get to bed early."

"Twenty-four hours!"

"That's standard for firefighters. But then we get two days off."

No wonder he had so much free time. "All right," Lorraine said. "I'll meet you now if you want."

"At the entrance to City Park?"

"I can be there in fifteen minutes."

"See you then."

Chapter 13

Lorraine approached the entrance to City Park, scanning the crowd of people milling about. It was a gorgeous day, and people were jogging, power walking, whizzing by on Rollerblades. A group of boys with skateboards under their arms ran past her. The addition of the skateboard park a few years ago had been a huge success.

The entrance to the park was packed with seniors, most with cameras in their hands. And that's when Lorraine saw Hunter. His back was to her as he was hunched over, apparently helping an older woman with her cell phone. He handed her back the phone, and the woman gripped his hand and smiled at him.

As Hunter stood tall, he turned. Within an instant, his eyes connected with hers. She waved, then started toward him.

He walked to meet her. His lips pulled in a grin when he neared her, but it didn't reach his eyes. She hadn't known him all that long, but it was clear to her that he was stressed.

"Thanks for coming," he said. "Sorry I had to go through your friend to get to you. I left yesterday without getting your number. And Joe's out of the office."

"Did you want to see me about the letter?" Lorraine asked.

"Among other things," Hunter said.

"Did you want to find a place in the park? Though it seems fairly busy to—"

The jolt to her body came out of the blue. She cried out as she was flung forward. Hunter's arms went around her instantly, catching her before she fell.

As Lorraine steadied herself in his arms, her brain registered what had happened to her. Someone had bumped into her. She followed Hunter's line of sight to the back of a teenager who was riding on his skateboard like a speed demon.

Hunter looked down at her, concern in his eyes. "You okay?"

Lorraine drew in a shaky breath. She nodded. "Yeah. How did that kid not see me?"

Hunter grimaced. "Some of these kids. I swear, it's like they're in their own world."

"Maybe we should sit outside of the park," she suggested as yet another kid on a skateboard whipped through the crowd. She pointed to a vacant bench near the road's edge, then started toward it.

Lorraine sat, and Hunter sat beside her. He looked out at the people passing by for several seconds before he spoke. "I used to come here with my dad. With my family. City Park was a favorite of ours."

Glancing at him, Lorraine nodded. "It's a beautiful spot."

"My mom used to love to go to the koi fish pond. Is it still there?"

"Oh, yeah. It's a favorite. Everyone loves going there to feed the fish."

"I never realized how much I missed this place until I returned," Hunter said softly.

"How long were you gone?"

"Sixteen years," he said, then glanced away. "I needed to get away."

"From your father?" Lorraine surmised.

Hunter nodded. Then he watched a young boy and his

father stroll by hand in hand. His jaw flinched. "I hope you've thought more about what I said yesterday," he said without facing her.

"Hunter…" Lorraine let out a soft sigh. "I really don't know about keeping the store."

Hunter faced her. "If I'd been some random guy you'd never met, would you be so ready to give up on your dream?"

She couldn't answer him, because the answer was obvious. So she asked a question of her own. "Why do you care what I do with my life?"

"Because I owe it to my father." Hunter lowered his head, his shoulders slumping. Lorraine could see the conflicting emotions in his body language. "I should have been there for my dad. I'm never going to get that time back. Even before I read his letter, that was eating at me." He paused. "And then when he gave you that gift… What he did made it clear to me that he was compassionate and kind, qualities I forced myself to believe he lacked. I've been trying to process so much, but the one thing I'm certain about is that his dying wish was to help you. And that's why I want you to keep his gift, Lorraine. Because of my father."

An unexpected wave of emotion washed over her. She felt for this man, who was clearly hurting because he'd lost his dad. She wanted to not care, but she couldn't.

The Hunter she'd met in the bar had stoked her desire. The one she'd met in the lawyer's office had made her feel lower than dirt. Right now, this one was exposing his vulnerability. He was laying his heart bare for her, and Lorraine felt her defenses lowering.

"Just…think about it," he said.

"All right," Lorraine said softly. "I won't make a decision yet. With Joe out of town, I can't, anyway."

She paused, and looked at him until he met her gaze.

"Whatever your father said in the letter, and whatever happened in your relationship with him, please, stop beating yourself up. I can see that you're hurting. What I said to you... The truth is, I was out of line. I don't know what happened between you and your dad. I don't know the dynamics of your relationship. It wasn't right for me to get on your case for not being there for him."

"But I should have been."

"Your father loved you, Hunter. I could tell he was torn up about the distance between both of you, but he never once blamed you for it. I said what I did because...well, because I was hurt by what you thought about me. But I'm happy to put that behind me if you are. Please, let's just wipe the slate clean."

Hunter's jaw tightened. He said nothing.

"Do you want to talk about it?" she asked gently.

Hunter turned away from her. He was in pain, that much was obvious. Why had he called her here if he didn't want to talk?

She put a gentle hand on his back. He drew in a heavy breath, and after a few seconds he turned to face her.

"Thank you," he said. "For what you said about my father. That means a lot."

"For what it's worth, I really liked him. He seemed genuinely like a good guy to me."

Hunter's eyes suddenly narrowed. "You were close. I'm surprised I didn't see you at the funeral."

"I got tired of reading obituaries a long time ago. I prefer to remember my patients as I knew them. I hate funerals."

"Who doesn't?"

"Plus I feel weird about going to the funerals of my patients. I don't want to intrude on a family's intimate grief."

"I get it." Hunter paused. "It was small, just at the funeral home. Me, a couple of my dad's family from out of state."

"So he had more family than the brother he was on bad terms with?" Lorraine asked.

"Yeah, there were more. He wasn't close to them. I'm surprised they showed up."

"They should have shown up while he was alive. Sorry—I should keep my opinion to myself. It's just… Your dad had no one."

"He had you."

Lorraine's eyes widened when she met Hunter's gaze, and he offered her a small smile. "That's sweet of you to say."

"All any of us can do is try to learn from the past. I think my dad had a habit of keeping things inside. He'd rather be quiet than confrontational. The problem is, it made him seem aloof, uncaring."

"And you don't think that now?"

Hunter shook his head. "No. Not anymore." He pursed his lips, deep in thought. Then he asked, "You want to see where he's buried?"

The question came out of the blue. And yet, it was something that had crossed Lorraine's mind before. That if she knew where Douglas was buried—*if* he'd been buried— she wouldn't mind paying her respects.

"Unexpected question, I know. But I feel like going there right now. Would you like to go with me?"

"Wouldn't you rather be alone?" Lorraine asked.

"I'd rather you come with me." Hunter shrugged. "You're the last one who spent any real time with my father. I mean, unless you don't want to."

"Actually, I'd very much like to know where he's been laid to rest."

"You want to go in my car, or follow me? It's the cemetery across town."

"I'll follow you," Lorraine said.

* * *

Half an hour later, Lorraine pulled into St. Joseph's Cemetery behind Hunter. A couple of times during the drive, she thought she would lose him when a car or two slipped in front of her. But she'd still been able to see Hunter's sleek BMW and catch up with him without incident.

St. Joseph's Cemetery was large and vast and sloped up the hillside. It spanned at least a few acres, and for Lorraine to try to find Douglas's grave in here would have been near impossible.

Hunter took his time driving along the narrow road that wound through the graveyard. Large oaks and other trees lined much of the roads and perimeter of the property, providing shade. Hunter slowed as he neared a number of cars parked along the edge of the gravel road and the grass. A funeral was in progress. Lorraine glanced to the right, taking in the sight of the mourners dressed in black, many of them with arms around each other for support.

Lorraine swallowed, thoughts of her own mother's funeral three years earlier filling her mind. The familiar sense of sadness, coupled with the undeniable anger, came rushing back. Her mother, who'd been diabetic, had made huge gains healthwise years ago, only to return to her old ways in her later years when she'd lost her willpower. Her mother had started saying things like "You can't live forever" and "May as well enjoy the one life you have." But while she'd said those words, Lorraine was pretty certain that her mother hadn't expected to die at fifty-six. And surely if she had known the void she would leave in the lives of those who'd loved her, she would have taken her health more seriously. She'd told a friend about the flu-like and nausea symptoms she was experiencing, but not Lorraine, probably because she knew that Lorraine would have lectured her mother about eating right. Unfortunately, those symptoms were precursors to the fact that her blood sugar was out of whack. Her mother had lapsed into a diabetic coma, and living alone after her divorce, no one had been able to help her.

Hunter slowed his car and stopped, and Lorraine pulled up behind him. She drew in a deep breath, trying to clear her mind of the memories of her mother's senseless and preventable tragedy. Of course, that wasn't easy to do when she was at the cemetery where her own mother was buried.

Hunter got out of his vehicle and started onto the grass. There was a fresh mound of dirt topped with a bouquet of white roses about ten feet away.

Lorraine exited her car, watching Hunter steadfastly. He didn't even glance over his shoulder as he made his way over to the new grave.

He stood there looking down at the fresh dirt, as if he couldn't believe that his father was in there. Lorraine knew the feeling. She stood beside him, saying nothing.

"There's no headstone yet," Hunter said. "Just a marker. I'm having something designed for my dad, but I'm not 100 percent sure yet what to put on it. I was thinking perhaps a verse that he liked." He looked at Lorraine. "I thought that maybe you could give me an idea?"

"Me?" she asked, unable to hide her shock.

"Did my dad ever share any Bible passages that meant anything to him?"

"No," Lorraine said. "Sorry."

"You mentioned he liked you reading to him. Any particular books?"

As she looked down at the white roses and fresh dirt, something came to her. "Actually, there's something your father said to me more than once. Now that I think about it, it must have meant something to him. He was reading the teachings of Buddha. He was dying, and I guess he was searching for some sort of spiritual enlightenment. Anyway, he quoted this more than once—'No matter how hard the past, you can always begin again.' I thought he was talking to me about my marriage, how it had fallen apart and I'd gone through hard times. But maybe those words meant something to him? Maybe the only thing standing between him and beginning again was the fact that his time was running out."

Lorraine saw Hunter's Adam's apple rise and fall. His eyes closed for a moment too long. Then he said, "My dad had reached out to me. He left me a few messages. Didn't say why, just asked me to call him. He never told me he was sick. Maybe he was trying to start again." Hunter's voice cracked slightly. "I denied him that."

"More than once, you said that your father didn't tell you he was sick. But you visited him at the hospice, didn't you?"

Hunter's expression was grim as he nodded. "I was called by staff at the hospice when his condition took a turn for the worse. It seems kind of crazy, because when I found out, I immediately quit my job and returned home. Suddenly, I was ready to be there for him, but what took me so long? That haunts me now."

"At least you got to see him before he died. Be grateful for that."

Hunter looked at her askance. "You've lost someone close to you?" he asked.

"Yeah. My mother."

"How long ago?"

"Three years. Diabetes eventually claimed my mother's life."

Hunter looked at her in confusion. "I thought you said that she was cured of her diabetes."

"She was. Until she wasn't. And that's what makes her death harder to accept." Lorraine looked toward the members of the funeral party. They were beginning to disperse. "Maybe she was depressed. She didn't want to live alone, so she let her health slide. I'll never really know because she didn't speak to me about it." Lorraine faced Hunter again. "Sometimes, even when you are on speaking terms with a loved one, they don't tell you everything. My mom ultimately slipped into a diabetic coma, and no one was there to get her out of it. I only found out later from a neighbor that she complained about feeling flu-like off and on for a number of months. But she didn't go to the doctor. Hell, if she wouldn't go to a doctor, she could have at least come to me. I'm a nurse, for heaven's sake. When I think about it, it infuriates me. She had complications with diabetes before. Why didn't she consider the possibility again? But no matter how upset I get, it won't change anything for her."

"That's why you want to help others so badly, isn't it? Because of your mother?"

"Yeah," Lorraine said softly.

Hunter slipped his arm around her waist and pulled her against his side. "I'm sorry," he said.

Despite the seriousness of their conversation, her skin warmed where he was touching her. Hunter was incredibly sexy, and everything about him drew her to him.

"Thanks," Lorraine said.

Hunter released her and looked down at his father's grave once more. "I had a twin sister. She died in a fire."

Lorraine's eyes flew to his. "Oh, Hunter. I'm so sorry."

"She was sleeping over at a friend's place. And that night of all nights, the house burned down. No smoke detectors. They all died."

"Oh, my God."

"We had the perfect family until then. Then everything went to hell. My parents became distant, my dad was closed off emotionally. Then my mom died a few years later and my dad got involved with another woman almost immediately, some young woman he tried to bring into the house to be a surrogate mother to me. I hated her. Well, maybe *hate* is a strong word, but I truly resented her and wanted nothing to do with her. And I hated seeing my dad laugh with her and shut me out, as though all that mattered to him was his new life. It seemed to me he forgot about my mother and my sister, buried them, and that was that. Wiped his hands of them."

"I'm sure he didn't feel that way," Lorraine said. "But that must have been hard for you to deal with as a kid."

"It was. His relationship quickly ended. Lasted almost a year. I think that woman was just a gold digger who was looking for a house and a man to take care of her. She had no real interest in me—maybe because she could tell I didn't like her. Anyway, I was glad when it ended, but my dad quickly found another woman, and that really solidified for me the fact that I wasn't a priority in his life. It was like I didn't matter to him anymore."

"Or maybe when he looked at you he saw what he lost. His wife, your sister. Maybe he was doing everything in his power to escape that devastating reality."

"Yeah. That's pretty much what he told me in his letter." Hunter dropped onto his haunches and felt the fresh dirt with the tips of his fingers. Then he glanced over his shoulder at Lorraine. "It was something I considered when I got older. One day it kind of hit me, maybe my dad behaved the way he did because he couldn't cope. Or that was the only way he *could* cope. But he'd shut me out, pushed me away and had done nothing to try to make our relationship work. By the time I was eighteen, I was leaving Ocean City. He didn't try to make me stay. In fact, when I told him I was leaving, he made plans to move in his current girlfriend. The way I saw it, he was happy for me to be gone."

"He said he had a lot of regrets in his life. I'm sure he

was talking about you, your mother and your sister, and how he handled everything."

"Maybe he was." Hunter stood. "It was hard for me. I was young, and I needed my father. And the bottom line is he wasn't there."

"Sadly, he paid the ultimate price for his actions. He died without you at his side. But I'm sure it meant the world to him that you saw him before he passed."

"I just wish he'd told me he'd been sick when it would have made a difference. When we would have had more time." He exhaled sharply. "But at least he wrote me this letter. It answered a lot of questions."

"Then I'm glad you got the closure you needed."

Lorraine's stomach tightened as she felt a wave of emotion. She understood the pain Hunter was going through. Losing a parent was crushing, and in this situation she could just imagine it was even worse. She'd felt devastated—and angry, to be honest—when her mother had passed. Ultimately, she felt that she had failed her. That she hadn't spent enough time with her. That her new marriage had caused her to neglect her mother in some way.

"I got married a year before my mother died," Lorraine said, feeling the need to share this fact with Hunter. "I saw my mother less and less. Talked to her less and less. We were close, and yet I still wasn't there for her when she was getting sicker. So I know exactly what it's like to lose someone you love and have regrets."

"I think we both need to forgive ourselves." Hunter placed his hands on his hips. "Mind if I have a few minutes alone with my dad?"

"Absolutely not. In fact, I'll just go—"

"No. Don't leave. Not yet."

Lorraine opened her mouth to protest, but she decided against it. Instead, she made her way to her car and got inside. She waited, as he'd asked her to do.

Though a huge part of her wanted to drive away. She was spending way too much time with Hunter.

The more she spent time with him and got to know him, the more she wanted to. She couldn't deny the chemistry between them, which only made her remember how good they'd been in the bedroom. And that was exactly the problem. Hunter was supposed to have been a one-night stand. Things had gotten complicated because of the fact that he was Douglas's son, and she wanted to uncomplicate them by giving him back the store and moving on with her life.

And yet, as she looked in his direction where he once again was on his haunches at the graveside, she felt a little tug in her heart. And if she were honest with herself, she knew that she wasn't really ready to be rid of him yet.

Chapter 14

Hunter's throat was clogged with emotion as he looked down at the dirt patch beneath which his father's body was buried. He felt cheated. All these years without his dad, and now there would be no more time.

He told his dad how he felt. That he was angry that he hadn't been a good father to him, and that he wished most of all they'd had this conversation while he was alive. "You needed to hear me tell you how hurt I was. Because maybe then you would have had the guts to tell me to my face what you wrote in that letter. Because that's what I needed to hear from you, more than anything."

Hunter was silent for a long moment. He drew in deep breaths, regaining his composure. Even though his father was gone, it was still hard letting his feelings out.

Hunter jerked when he felt the hands on his shoulders. He whipped his head up and saw Lorraine there, looking down at him. Her eyes were filled with tears, and compassion was evident on her contorted face. She got down onto her knees beside him. "I'm sorry. I know you said for me to stay in the car, but I could see you were in pain. And…"

Hunter drew her into his arms and hugged her. He held on. He held on as the emotion roared inside him. He held her tightly as he thought of his dad and the regret. He wanted this to be it, right here, right now. No more grief over his dad and the losses in his life. No more grieving over unresolved pain. After today, he wanted to be able to think of his father and remember him fondly.

He finally released Lorraine. Shakily, he got to his feet, then helped pull Lorraine to a standing position. His emotions were raw, overwhelming in a way he didn't expect. But amidst the chaos of the anger and the regret and guilt and grief he felt a spark of hope.

A seagull squawked as it flew overhead at that moment, and Hunter quickly looked up. The tension left his shoulders as a laugh bubbled up in his throat.

His sign?

"Are you okay?" Lorraine asked him, wiping at her eyes.

"I think I just got a sign that all's going to be okay," Hunter said.

Lorraine narrowed her eyes. "What do you mean?"

"You'd have to know the story," Hunter said, the memory filling him with warmth. "There used to be this seagull in our backyard. Decided to make our yard its home. Built a nest there and everything. My dad tried all he could to get the bird to go away without hurting it, but it kept coming back. He'd spray it with water, he would chase it until it flew away. But the darn thing kept coming back. And then one day there were babies in the nest. For a moment, my dad contemplated getting rid of them. But my mother pleaded with him not to, so he didn't. And now a seagull just flew overhead as I thought to myself that I want to finally have a sense of peace about my dad. It feels like a sign. The kind of sign my dad would send to make me smile."

Lorraine's face twisted with emotion at his words. "That's the sweetest thing I think I've heard."

He pulled her into his arms again and held her. He didn't know why she felt like a rock to him at this moment, but right now he needed her.

"Will you go back to my place with me?"

Her eyes widened, those beautiful eyes that had caught his attention in the bar. Bright. Hopeful and yet wary.

"Not for long," Hunter went on. "We can watch a mov maybe. I don't know. I just don't want to be alone rig now."

Lorraine didn't answer right away, and he could see th discomfort in her eyes. She'd gone from being a one-nig stand to suddenly being something else to him. A friend

"I don't really have any other friends in Ocean City, he told her. "There are a few guys from the station, bu no one...close. If you have something else to do, it's fine I just thought... I can even make some dinner or pic something up. It's the least I can do to repay you for bein here for me."

"You don't have to repay me. I was happy to come here I wanted to see where your father was buried. I really di like your dad," Lorraine said, her voice cracking slightly "I'm so sorry he's gone."

Hunter slipped an arm around her shoulder. "Yeah. Me. too." He paused. "Come by. Let me cook you dinner."

"All right," Lorraine agreed. "I'll come by for a little while."

Why did I agree to this? Lorraine asked herself after Hunter handed her a green smoothie. *This is a mistake.*

Already she was looking at Hunter differently. She was seeing him as the sexy, irresistible man she'd met at the bar. And remembering their explosive passion once they'd gotten to his place.

"Kale, mango, pineapple and a bit of spinach," he said. "I hope that's okay."

"It's fine," Lorraine said, and took a sip. "It tastes great, thank you."

She watched Hunter walk back into the kitchen, checking out his behind. His strong thighs. She quickly drank more of her smoothie.

It had been the plea in his voice, the clear fact that he'd

needed her after he'd read his father's letter that had her saying yes to this time together at his place. Her relationship with Hunter had been like a roller coaster ever since they'd met, and she was still on the ride.

The first night, they'd connected sexually in a way that had excited her more than anyone before him. Unexpectedly, loss had brought them together again. Today had been especially draining, but Lorraine couldn't bring herself to leave him when he needed her.

Hunter joined her in the living room with his own green smoothie. He offered her a small smile. "Thank you. For being with me today."

"No problem," Lorraine said. "I'm glad I got to see your father's grave. You don't mind if I visit it some time, bring some flowers?"

"Of course not."

"Great." She finished off her smoothie. "I know I said I'd hang out for a bit, but I really ought to get going."

"Already?" Hunter asked. "I offered you dinner, remember? We can even watch a movie, escape reality for a while."

Lorraine bit down on her bottom lip. "I don't know, Hunter."

"Besides, it's my dad's birthday today."

Lorraine's mouth fell open in surprise. "It is?"

Hunter nodded. "Yep. Would have been sixty-three."

"Why didn't you say something?"

He shrugged. "Because it's always been a bittersweet day. And even more so now that he's gone. You being with me today...you helped me get some perspective and some closure. I don't know. It suddenly seems appropriate to mark the occasion with some dinner, maybe a drink to toast him. I'd like to turn the tide and end the day smiling. It seems fitting that you be here with me to do that, given how close you and my father got."

If that wasn't an emotional tug on her heartstrings, noth-ing was. Lorraine literally couldn't find a reason to say no

"You know how to twist a girl's arm."

"I can order pizza. There's a place nearby that make it with a gluten-free crust, and I get it margherita-style with no cheese and lots of veggies, a good dose of basil and some olive oil. They also make pasta from brown rice which is healthier. But it's up to you. You want something else, we can do that, too. I typically try to eat a very clean diet, but I allow myself some cheat days."

"A cheeseless pizza with veggies is your idea of a cheat day?" Lorraine asked, a smile touching her lips. "That sounds pretty darn healthy if you ask me."

"Cheat days is a big, juicy cheeseburger with all the toppings. You know that burger chain, Jordan's Burger Shack?"

"I've never been in there," Lorraine admitted. "But I know they're popular in California."

"And Nevada. They make the best burgers. Huge, greasy, tasty. And a ton of calories, which is why I only have one there maybe twice a year. I love the meathead burger. A full pound and a half of beef, topped with cheese, bacon and onion rings. I get it with a side order of sweet potato fries. I wash it all down with a Coors."

"Sounds like quite the meal."

"Tastes amazing at the time, but, man, the aftermath." Hunter made a face. "I never feel good the next day. I typically stay away from red meat. Like I said, I try to eat clean."

"For me, it's potato chips. Salt and vinegar, ketchup, dill pickle or just plain. I crave salts for my comfort foods."

"So I just have to pick up a couple of bags of potato chips for dinner?" Hunter asked, grinning.

"I'll need more than that," Lorraine told him. "The

pizza you described sounds delicious to me. And gluten-free pasta in plain tomato sauce?"

"Works for me," Hunter said. "Are you into suspense? I brought a box of DVDs from my dad's place, and those ones were his favorite. We can pick one."

"Sure," she said. Though the truth was, a lot of good suspense movies scared her. "If that's what your father liked, why not watch one for his birthday?"

Hunter smiled. "I'll order the pizza. You pick a movie from the box beside the TV. Any veggies you don't like?"

"Nope. I'm good with them all."

An hour and a half later, the mostly eaten pizza was on the coffee table in front of them, along with two empty wine glasses.

And now a thriller starring Liam Neeson was playing on the television. The scares seemed even more intense with Lorraine watching them on a fifty-inch screen. She almost felt as though she were a part of the terror.

"Oh, God," she uttered when a gun battle began. The surround sound only made things worse. It literally sounded like bullets were whizzing by her ears.

She put a hand over her eyes, splaying her fingers to peek out at the horrifying action.

The feel of the hand on her leg caused her heart to slam against her rib cage. Jerking her leg away, she screamed.

"Hey," Hunter said. He looked at her with concern. "You're really scared."

"I—I should have told you that I can get freaked out during suspense movies."

Hunter shuffled his body across the sofa, filling up the space Lorraine had deliberately left vacant. "You want me to turn it off?"

She felt silly. She knew these movies weren't real, but

the scares were so real, she couldn't help reacting. "I'll be fine," she told him.

He slipped his arm around her shoulder and drew her close. "Come here."

He pulled her against his body, and despite herself, Lorraine immediately felt safer in his strong arms. Not only was she a wimp when it came to scary movies, she was a pathetic cliché, needing a man to make her feel better.

"I can turn it off," Hunter said.

On the screen, the gun battle had just ended, and Liam Neeson was victorious. "No," Lorraine said. "Let's watch it."

Though the scary moment had passed, Hunter continued to hold her. He moved his hand from her shoulder to her arm, where his fingers brushed her skin. Lorraine's pulse began to race—and not because of the movie this time.

Hunter's fingers skimmed her skin, soft caresses. Lorraine's pulse was thundering in her ears to the point where she could no longer register the dialogue on the screen.

"Better?" Hunter asked.

She looked at him, smiling feebly. "Yeah."

He didn't look away. And neither did she. Lorraine's breath caught in her throat when she felt the decided shift between them. As Hunter urged her closer, suddenly the movie was simply background noise.

"I'm glad you're here," he whispered.

Did his voice have to sound so incredibly sexy? And the way he was looking at her. Was that all it took to get her aroused? A look and a touch?

Obviously.

"Damn it," Hunter uttered.

"What?" Lorraine asked, her voice barely audible.

"I don't even care about the movie anymore."

She didn't have to ask what he *did* care about.

The way his hand was smoothing up and down her arm made that obvious.

And suddenly, it was what she cared about, too.

If only he would stop touching her, maybe she would be able to think clearly.

"I…I should probably…go," she managed to say. "You have to go to bed early."

Hunter's eyes widened. "You want to leave?"

No, she didn't *want* to leave. But the part of her brain that was still working knew that she *needed* to leave—unless she wanted to end up naked with Hunter again. And wasn't that the last thing she wanted?

He was stroking her arm with one hand, and with the other one he linked fingers with hers. "I don't want you to go."

Oh, God…

Just yesterday, she'd planned to sign over the store to Hunter and be done with him once and for all. How on earth was she here with him, *wanting* him so desperately?

Hunter brushed his lips against her cheek. "Don't go, Lorraine. Please, stay."

The deep timbre of his voice washed over her skin like a languid caress. And Lord help her, Lorraine was powerless to say no.

Chapter 15

Lorraine looked into Hunter's eyes. The desire she saw in their dark depths caused her breath to catch in her throat. He wanted her—and she couldn't deny that she wanted him.

Yet somehow she managed to say, "This...this wasn't the plan." Her voice sounded thick, and she cleared her throat before continuing. "Today is about your father."

Hunter nuzzled his nose against her cheek. "I think my father would approve."

Heat spread along Lorraine's skin. She couldn't even refute that. She'd known that Douglas had really liked her. She couldn't imagine him objecting to her getting involved with his son.

"This wasn't in the plans...for us. I mean, things are complicated." Lorraine didn't even understand her own words. Was she even speaking English?

"Were you planning to head home with me when you met me at the bar?" Hunter asked.

"What?" Lorraine's eyes narrowed. "Why are you asking me that?"

"Because sometimes you just have to go with the flow. Live life in the moment. Like we did that night in the bar. I didn't have ulterior motives in mind when I invited you here. I only wanted the company, not to spend my father's birthday alone. But being this close to you..." He tightened his fingers on hers. "Damn."

Lorraine swallowed. Why was she so aroused? Just

being near Hunter was an assault on her sanity. All reason fled her mind.

"When I'm close to you, all I think about is touching you. Yesterday, when you were telling me about your vision for the store, I wanted so badly to kiss you."

"What?" He had? But was she really surprised? She'd felt the pull of attraction between them then, too. The truth was, she'd never *not* felt it, no matter how angry she wanted to be with him.

"You were telling me about your dream, and... I don't know. I found your passion really sexy."

Even though her pulse was racing, Lorraine said, "Come on."

Hunter reached for the remote control and turned the movie off. "You're hella sexy, Lorraine. You must know that."

"Not really," she said, and wondered why she was admitting that to him.

Hunter's eyebrows shot up. "Your husband didn't tell you you were sexy?"

He had, in the beginning. But not for the longest time. In fact, Lorraine had felt more like a burden to him than anything else.

Hunter took her silence as confirmation. "Then the man needs to have his head examined. Lorraine, you take my breath away."

The last of her resistance slipped away. "You win," she whispered.

"I win? You think this a game to me?"

"If it is, you don't play to lose."

"I'm just mad attracted to you," he said. "Am I the only one feeling this?"

Maybe it was the vulnerable hitch to his voice, the rawness of emotion she heard. Maybe it was the earnest look in his eyes. The look that said he was unable to control whatever it was that seemed to have him in its grip. She understood. Because she felt the same way, too.

Lorraine repositioned herself on the sofa so that her legs were beneath her and her body was facing Hunter's. "I feel it, too," she admitted. He had put himself out on an emotional ledge, and she didn't want to leave him there alone. To make him believe that she wasn't as interested in him as he was in her would have been dishonest and cruel. God only knew why she was attracted to him, but she was. Fiercely.

Hunter wrapped his brawny arms around her and held her like that for a long while. He stroked her back, his fingers going round and round in lazy circles. Lorraine wanted him to kiss her, and yet he was simply staring into her eyes, drawing out the tension between them.

"Why aren't you kissing me?" she whispered, being uncharacteristically bold.

"Because I like looking at you. I love your bright eyes. And your lips." He ran a finger along her bottom lip. "God, you're beautiful."

Lorraine drew in a deep breath, then bit down on her bottom lip after Hunter lifted his finger. He was saying all the right things.

"And I like that, too," he whispered. "The way you bite your lip like that when you want me to kiss you."

Did she? "I don't do that."

"You did it a lot that first night."

Her body flushed. She wasn't sure she could handle any more of this verbal foreplay. She was dying for him to kiss her, touch her, take her clothes off and give her another incredible night.

Finally, Hunter edged his face toward hers, slowly—drawing out the tension even more. When Lorraine mewled softly in protest, his lips pulled into a grin. He was enjoying this!

"Hunter…" she pleaded.

"I know, baby." And then his arms tightened around her, and finally his lips came down on hers, and *goodness*, the electrical charge that hit her body was intense. She drew in a gasp even as he kissed her. And then she gripped his shoulders, hanging on to him as if he were a lifeline as his lips moved over hers slowly and oh so hotly. She opened her mouth, giving him more access, and his tongue instantly swept across hers.

Hunter slipped his hands beneath her shirt, and she wrapped her arms around his neck. She was caught in a storm of passion that was raging with the power of a tornado. Their mouths were mating hungrily, his hands splaying over her back and moving up and down and pressing her body against his hard chest. She dug her fingers into his shoulders as dizzying sensations made her light-headed with desire. She was breathing heavily, her body wildly alive. She hadn't felt this good since…

Since the last time she'd been in his arms.

Hunter broke the kiss and gazed at her. "You drive me crazy, you know that?" he whispered hotly.

"Don't stop," Lorraine begged. She snaked her arm around the back of Hunter's head and pulled it down, forcing their lips to meet again. She didn't want his lips to leave hers. Not now, not ever.

It was an irrational thought, of course, and yet everything about him touching her made her feel right. Made her feel amazing. She didn't want it to end.

He ground out a sound of passion, and it turned her on even more. Made her feel as though she had the power of his pleasure in her hands. Slipping his hands around to the front of her body, he suckled her bottom lip. Lorraine whimpered with pleasure.

"Yes," Hunter rasped in response to her wanton passion. He eased his body away from hers, and Lorraine moaned in protest. She didn't want him to stop touching her. "Don't you worry, baby," he told her, grinning down at her with the sexiest expression she'd ever seen.

He smoothed his hands over her belly, crisscrossing them back and forth. Lorraine swallowed. Then he undid the clasp on her jeans. The way he was looking at her with an intense, unwavering gaze stoked her inner fire. His eyes were as electrifying as his touch.

He pulled at the jeans, and she lifted her hips to make it easier for him to pull them off her legs. He took his time, as though removing her pants was an art form. He dropped the jeans onto the floor, then took one of her legs in his hands. He kissed the side of her calf, letting his lips linger. His mouth sent tingles of pleasure shooting along her skin.

Lorraine's breathing became shallow. Hunter kissed a path up her leg, trilling her belly with the tips of his fingers as he did. Then his hand went higher, covering her breast. Just one stroke over her nipple and it hardened against the lacy material of her bra.

Hunter moved his head from her inner thigh to her stomach, where his hand had recently been. He kissed her skin softly, then dipped his tongue into her belly button.

Lorraine arched her back and moaned.

"Baby," Hunter rasped. He slipped his fingers into the sides of her underwear and slowly pulled it down over her legs.

Lorraine's breathing came in short gasps. Here she was, lying on the sofa, her body almost fully exposed. The lights were dim, but still bright enough to leave nothing to the imagination. Unlike their first night together, when they'd made love in the darkness. She was far more vulnerable like this, and yet the way Hunter was looking at her, with unbridled passion and appreciation, made her feel more powerful than vulnerable.

He went onto his knees on the floor beside the sofa,

then ran a hand along her leg. "Perfect legs," he said. His eyes narrowed on her womanhood, the part of her body where she most craved his touch. "Perfect...*mmm*." He moved his hand up her thigh and over her stomach, then beneath her loose shirt. He tweaked one nipple, then the other. Lorraine's eyes fluttered shut.

"Turn over for me, baby," Hunter whispered.

Lorraine turned onto her stomach, and Hunter first smoothed his hands over her behind, then up her back. When he reached her bra, he undid the clasp. And then his lips, soft and tantalizing, were kissing the skin that had just been exposed.

Lorraine's skin was tingling, her pulse pounding. "You're killing me," she said.

"No, I'm teasing you." He slipped a hand beneath her body and pulled her toward him, turning her as he did. He positioned her so that she was sitting on the sofa in front of him. "Raise your arms."

She did as instructed, and Hunter lifted her shirt off her body. Then he dragged her bra straps over her shoulders and down her arms.

"I just want to look at you," Hunter uttered, his eyes roaming over her breasts like a warm caress. "It made me crazy when I got up and you were gone. I wanted more of you." Placing his hands on her thighs, he leaned forward to softly kiss her lips. "Of this."

Lorraine was fully naked, completely vulnerable and totally turned on.

Gently, Hunter guided her legs apart. Easing backward, his eyes greedily took in the sight of her breasts, then went lower, to her center. With a hand, he followed the route his eyes had taken. Lorraine gasped in pleasure when he fondled her most sweet spot. His fingers on her moist skin had her blood rushing faster.

"Oh, Hunter..." Lorraine arched her back as a delicious onslaught of sensations attacked her body. He slipped his finger inside her, and when Lorraine moaned, Hunter growled. Then he brought his mouth down on to her nipple and suckled her. The dual sensations of his fingers and his mouth had heat spiraling through her body in delicious waves.

He sucked her nipple deeper into his mouth, and Lorraine's limbs grew weak. She dug her hands into Hunter's shoulders and hung on.

He moved his mouth to her other breast and ran his tongue slowly around her areola. Round and round, until Lorraine was panting, her body on sensory overload.

"Lie back," he told her, pressing his palm between her breast bone and urging her backward. He kissed a path down her belly, and kept going lower. Lorraine sucked in a breath in anticipation and held it. And then his tongue began to tease her with soft flicks and gentle suckles, and her breath oozed out of her on a loud sigh. Lorraine's head dropped backward against the sofa, her limbs turning liquid against the delicious onslaught of Hunter's tongue.

"Yes… Oh, my God…"

She grabbed clumpfuls of Hunter's shirt, holding on as the pleasure rolled through her body. She gasped his name, dug her fingers into his shoulders—wanton and needy and shameless. His mouth picked up speed, greedily suckling. The tension was building, like a spring being wound.

And then the spring broke free, and Lorraine was vaulted into that most delicious abyss. She cried out, her moan long and unabashed. Hunter was making her feel alive again and incredibly amazing. She arched her back, luxuriating in these feelings.

"Yes," Hunter rasped, stroking her with his fingers, drawing out her climax.

"I need you…inside me."

Hunter grabbed each side of his shirt in his fists and

ripped it open with one strong pull. Buttons went flying, and Lorraine bit down on her bottom lip as a rush of fresh heat flooded through her. She loved that Hunter wanted her so badly that he wasn't even stopping to unbutton his shirt. Then she smiled, remembering how he'd said that she always bit her bottom lip when she wanted to be kissed.

He was right. She wanted to wrap her naked body around him and kiss him as he filled her with his manhood.

Hunter shrugged out of his shirt as fast as possible, as if the fabric was burning his skin.

He was gorgeous. His body was perfectly sculpted, his muscles the product of hard work in the gym.

The shirt discarded, Hunter got to his feet and undid his belt, then pants. Lorraine watched him, her eyes greedily taking in his strong legs and his white boxer briefs. His erection strained against the fabric, large and impressive. She hadn't been able to truly check his body out last week because they'd come together in a flurry of fast and hot passion in his darkened bedroom. Now, they were taking their time—and she was enjoying the show as he disrobed for her.

Hunter winked, and again Lorraine bit down on her bottom lip. "I know, baby. I want to kiss you, too. But I admit, I'm enjoying checking out your gorgeous body. Looking at you lying on the sofa like that… Damn."

"Get naked already," Lorraine commanded, then smiled playfully. And when he slowly pulled the briefs down his thighs, she sucked in a sharp breath.

Oh, wow. Hunter was absolutely stunning. Absolutely everything. He was the hottest man she'd ever been naked with, the one man who'd thrilled her beyond anyone else, and here she was about to make love to him again. He was the epitome of a fantasy come to life.

He took her by the hand, urging her up. And then he

scooped her into his arms. His mouth claimed hers as he carried her to his bedroom.

Desire shot through her body like liquid heat, while at the same time an unexpected sensation of warmth filled her heart. Hunter was gorgeous, yes—but he was also a decent guy. And their explosive sexual connection couldn't have felt more natural.

Hunter placed her on the bed, then put on a condom. As he settled between her legs, the veracity of that connection hit her full force. It was like a living, tangible thing, ensnaring both her and Hunter in its grip.

Hunter kissed her, a languid and deep kiss, making her light-headed. She wrapped a leg around his massive thigh as he guided his shaft inside her.

He filled her inch by delicious inch. Lorraine wrapped her arms around him as intense, sweet pleasure shot through her. And he was still kissing her, his mouth creating its own sensual assault while his shaft thrust deep inside her. She held on, loving the feel of his hard chest against her breasts, his tongue inside her mouth, his strong body between her thighs.

They clung to each other, their bodies moving slowly. This was unlike their first time, when their coupling was fast and frenzied. Hunter's tongue swept through her mouth with broad, sensual strokes while he raised a hand to her face and gently caressed her cheek. The tips of his fingers created delicious tingles on her skin. Lorraine locked her legs around his waist and raised her hips to meet each of Hunter's thrusts. And Lord, the sensations…

In his arms, Lorraine was transported to a different world. A world where she had no cares or concerns other than right here, right now. Nothing mattered more than giving and receiving pleasure with this man.

Hunter finally broke the kiss and moved his lips to her ear. His fingers still trilling her skin, he sucked her lobe between his lips and began to suckle the flesh. Softly, like he'd done with her most erogenous zones. And, oh, the sensation of his lips and teeth on her earlobe combined with the way he was moving deeply inside her caused the pleasure to intensify. Another climax was building.

"Hunter..." she rasped.

"I know, baby." He pulled his head back and gazed into her eyes, and something mystical and confounding washed over her. Lorraine stroked his face, her fingertips brushing against stubble. She couldn't help feeling that they had connected beyond the physical.

"I'm there, too," Hunter whispered hotly. He thrust deeply, burrowing himself inside her. "I'm right with you, baby."

And the lustful hitch in his voice, the feel of him buried deep within her and the way he was staring into her eyes pushed her over the edge.

"Oh, God… Hunter…"

"Yes!" Hunter growled, his muscles growing taut against her body. He eased back, then thrust deep and hard inside her, sending Lorraine's climax to the stratosphere. And as he buried his face in her neck and grunted, she knew that he was joining her in that magical place. A place of carnal bliss that they had created together.

They stayed like that for a long while, their harried breathing starting to subside, their bodies still physically connected. Lorraine's legs remained locked around Hunter's behind, his body still between her thighs. Her sense of contentment was so overwhelming that she never wanted to get up.

Hunter was the first to move. He kissed her shoulder blade, then her neck and then her cheek. "You okay?" he whispered in her ear.

"Fine." She was more than fine. She was perfect.

"You're amazing," he told her, then softly kissed her lips.

Lorraine's pulse tripped. How easily she could get used to this. Used to him in her life. Incredible sex with a gorgeous man. Who wouldn't?

Finally, Hunter eased back, kissing her lips softly before fully moving his body off hers. "Don't go anywhere," he said, and smiled.

"Where would I go?" Lorraine teased.

He gave her a pointed look, and she got his drift. She'd taken off that first night, and while he was joking, he was making a reference to the fact that he didn't want her taking off again.

But what *did* he want?

It doesn't matter what he wants, she told herself. Because no matter how amazing she felt in his arms, and in his presence, she didn't want to spend nights thinking about someone, wondering if he was going to call. Wondering if she was going to see him.

Wondering how long before their relationship failed.

Hunter wandered off to the bathroom, and Lorraine's heart pounded as she shamelessly stared at his perfectly chiseled body. Once he was around the corner and out of view, she sat up and searched for her clothes.

Lorraine's cell phone rang, and she jumped, startled. She was glad that the phone hadn't gone off while she'd been in the middle of making love to Hunter. She quickly scrambled for her purse and dug out her cell phone. She saw Rosa's face flashing on her screen.

Oh, no. She couldn't talk to Rosa right now, not while she was fresh from making love with Hunter and not even dressed yet. Lorraine swiped to reject the call.

Several seconds later, Lorraine's phone made a chirping sound, and she saw a message from Rosa pop up on her screen.

Did you just reject my call? Where are you and what are you up to???

Lorraine switched her phone to silent and dropped it back into her purse. She would have to explain everything to her friend later.

Hunter rounded the corner, naked and minus the condom, and Lorraine's eyes widened. Seeing him nude and in all his glory caught her off guard, though she should have expected that. It was just that he was so darn sexy. And she'd had two unforgettable escapades with him.

He bit down on his bottom lip as he looked at her, then winked and Lorraine got his point. "You want me to kiss you, don't you?"

"Hell, yeah, I want you to kiss me." He reached for her hands and pulled her to her feet, then planted a soft, lingering kiss on her lips.

The stirrings of desire started in her belly, and just like that, she knew she could spend all day and all night here with Hunter and not even blink an eye. How had this man so easily ensnared her in his sexual spell?

"I—I have to go," she blurted out. Her pulse was racing, her stomach tensing, a profound sense of anxiety hitting her with full force. Suddenly, she knew that she had to get out of there. She had to break this physical connection between her and Hunter, get away before she started caring.

His eyes narrowed in confusion as he looked at her. "You're leaving already?"

She stepped out of his embrace and averted her eyes from his spectacular body, or she might not be able to maintain her resolve to go. "I just got a call from a friend of mine. She's…having a crisis. When I didn't answer the call, she texted to say that she needs to talk to me urgently," Lorraine lied. "Besides, you need to get some rest.

You'll never do that with me here," she added with a wink to soften the blow.

Hunter slipped his arms around her waist and pulled her against his naked body. She sighed softly, wanting to melt against him and lose herself in the carnal sensations that were already starting to pulse through her again. She wanted to stay for more of what he had just given her. Maybe lie in bed with him all night and this time wake up next to him...

No, that was *not* what she wanted. So what if she'd had sex with a hot guy? Hadn't she fallen into that trap with her ex-husband? Their chemistry had started hot, and she'd mistaken that for love. Lorraine was painfully aware that sex didn't make a relationship.

"You know how to get a hold of me," Lorraine said. "We'll talk soon."

"All right, baby."

The word *baby* caused a frisson of heat to travel down her spine. She knew it was simply a lusty term of endearment after sex, but a small part of her felt like it actually meant something.

"At least this time you're not leaving me hanging." Hunter grinned down at her with that charming grin that had attracted her in the bar. There was no surprise as to why she'd been fiercely drawn to him.

"Now you'd better let me go so I can get dressed," Lorraine said.

"If I must," Hunter agreed, and released her. "But I'll see you soon, right?"

Lorraine offered him a small smile instead of a direct answer. Because she didn't know what to say. He wanted to spend more time with her, but Lorraine wasn't sure she wanted that.

In fact, the very notion terrified her.

Chapter 16

"I just have to make sure that I never see him again."

Lorraine raised her glass of water to her lips and took a swig. She was at Rosa's condo and sitting beside her on the sofa. She'd gone home only to shower, then had immediately gone to Rosa's place. She needed someone to talk to about this complicated situation.

"I saw the chemistry between you two the first night," Rosa said. "It's not rocket science that you two ended up doing the horizontal tango again."

Lorraine's face flushed hotly. "But I should know better. Once, I can understand. But twice?"

"You said he's quite the lover. It's clear to me that your body was down for another roll in the hay, even if your brain wasn't."

"Please, stop with all those sex metaphors," Lorraine said, then sighed. "Sorry. I'm not mad at you. I'm mad at myself." She sipped more water. "I totally planned to sign the store over to him, but then you had me thinking twice about it and when I spoke to Hunter about his father's wishes, I started to realize that maybe I was being hasty in making that decision. He suggested that we work together."

Rosa's eyes lit up.

"He said he's looking for a business opportunity, that this would be a way to honor his father."

"But…?" Rosa asked. "You think he's being dishonest?"

"No, not at all. In fact, I completely understand why that would appeal to him. He's wrestling with the reality that his father wasn't as bad as he thought, and he wants to do something meaningful to remember him."

"That's great. Isn't it?"

"It'd be great if I didn't think about getting naked every time I looked at him." Lorraine groaned. "Keeping the store will mean tethering myself to him even further. And I just… I don't want to be vulnerable to a guy like him."

"What does that mean?"

"You know. He's experienced. You don't get to be that great in the bedroom without a lot of experience."

"So you're *upset* that you two click sexually?"

"That's not what I'm saying. It's just… I don't want to set myself up to be hurt. You know my track record. I'm not good at casual sex. I've never gone to bed with someone I didn't know and like…until now. And after today with him, seeing his vulnerable side and connecting…" Lorraine's voice trailed off.

"You like him," Rosa supplied.

Lorraine swallowed. She *did* like him. And that was precisely the problem. Fresh from a relationship that had ripped her heart out and dealt a blow to her self-esteem, she wasn't ready to put herself in a vulnerable position again.

"I think I'll let some time pass, then contact the lawyer to finalize the paperwork to sign the store over to Hunter."

"You're not going to keep it?"

"After today… Come on, Rosa. You know I can't."

"The only thing I know is that you seem more frazzled than I've ever seen you before. But kind of in a good way."

Lorraine's eyebrows shot up. Rosa gave her a sly smile. "Your problem is that you're a hopeless romantic. I should have gone to see Amanda."

"But you didn't. You came to see me. The one person you knew would tell you to stop being afraid and just go for it. Why is that?"

Lorraine's lips parted, but she wasn't sure how to answer the question. Why *hadn't* she gone to see Amanda? Amanda had been burned by love and knew how to get involved without putting her heart on the line. Amanda would have told Lorraine to cut ties with Hunter—immediately.

"You know why," Lorraine said. "You and I have always been the closest." While Trina and Amanda were her friends for life as well, Rosa was like the sister Lorraine had always wanted.

"You like this guy, I can see that. And that's okay. But you're scared. After Paul, how could you not be?"

Rosa always saw the sexual attraction without the rest of the drama. She lived for that initial spark and the fantasy of happily-ever-after. Lorraine had been married, hurt and the last thing she was looking for was another relationship.

"Don't be afraid to love again," Rosa went on. "Maybe Hunter's the one."

Rosa's words played on Lorraine's mind all through that night and even the next day. She had to admit, she couldn't stop thinking about Hunter and their explosive chemistry. She'd spent much of the day driving around and checking out vacant properties, but the idea of keeping the store was preoccupying her thoughts. Especially after she'd received a text from Hunter bright and early, where he repeated what he'd told her the day before. His father would want her to keep the store; he would help her run it.

And his last words had truly touched her heart. *If wanting to spend more time with you is a crime, then I'm guilty.*

Lorraine had gone through the motions of checking out a few possible locations, asking neighboring business owners how they liked the area, but she was leaning toward doing what she never thought she would—keeping the store.

Her response to Hunter, however, had been reserved. She told him that she needed more time to consider what she would do, and that she didn't want their relationship to cloud her judgment.

Lorraine was determined to take her time and make the right decision. To weigh the pros and cons before deciding what she should do.

As she turned into her townhouse complex, she realized that once again, Hunter was consuming her thoughts. The truth was, she hadn't been able to stop thinking about him. Their time together yesterday had culminated in an amazing lovemaking experience. Hunter had opened up to her, been completely vulnerable about his father and their past, and Lorraine's walls around her heart had come crashing down. Yesterday had marked a shift within her. Hunter wasn't just a man with a spectacular body who could make her feel utterly amazing. He was a good man, with complex emotions. He was real—and Lorraine liked the person she was getting to know.

She parked in her usual spot in the townhouse parking lot, and made her way toward her unit. Maybe Rosa was right. And Hunter, too. Keeping the store would allow her to pursue her dream, and honor Douglas in the process. And if she got to know Hunter a little better…? Why was she letting her past dictate her future? He wasn't Paul, after all.

Lorraine halted before ascending the few steps to her door. A spectacular array of a dozen or so yellow lilacs with red highlights sat in a thick glass jar filled partly with water. Vibrant greens added to the lushness of the bouquet.

"Hunter," she said, and rushed toward the beautiful arrangement, her heart pounding. How many times had she said that she needed to put Hunter in the rearview mirror? Yet seeing that he'd sent her flowers had her heart filling with warmth.

With hope.

She searched for a card, an ear-to-ear smile dancing on

er lips. He must really like her. A guy wouldn't send a
ooty call flowers, would he?

Finding no card, Lorraine frowned. But after a few sec-
nds of confusion, she started to giggle. Hunter was try-
ng to be mysterious. She liked that.

Lorraine opened the door and took the stunning bouquet inside, where she placed it on her kitchen table. Only
as she was positioning the arrangement to best get the
ight did she wonder how Hunter had gotten her address.
Through the lawyer?

Not more than thirty seconds later, the doorbell rang. A
ush of excitement instantly ran through Lorraine's veins.

Hunter? But wasn't he working?

Maybe he had his whole squad on a firetruck and was
making a quick stop to see her. Lorraine grinned at the fan-
ciful thought. Rosa's romanticism was rubbing off on her.

She bounded toward the door, hopeful as she opened
it quickly.

"What are you—" The question died on her lips when
she saw who was standing outside her door. Her face crumbled.

Paul!

"What's the matter?" Paul asked, speaking with a tone
of mock concern. "I'm not who you expected?"

Lorraine swallowed, uncomfortable. Why was her ex-
husband here?

Paul gave her a creepy smile, then glanced beyond
her into her home. "You're not going to invite me in?"
he asked.

"What are you doing here?"

"Is that any way to greet me?" he asked.

"You're not welcome here."

"But we need to talk." And before Lorraine could protest, Paul pushed past her and walked into her townhouse.

"We have nothing to talk about," Lorraine said. "N
anymore."

"Oh, but we do. We need to talk about the divorce."

Lorraine's eyes narrowed. Was Paul drunk or simpl
out of his mind? "What's there to talk about? Everything
official."

"That's what I thought. Until I found out you weren
completely honest with me."

Lorraine crossed her arms over her chest and blew ou
a frustrated breath. "Paul, I don't have time for this."

He wandered into her kitchen, as though he owned th
place. "Nice flowers."

"All right, enough," Lorraine said. "Either tell me why
you came here or leave."

Paul made a dramatic show of sniffing one of the lilacs, then smiled. "Beautiful flowers. From a new man?"

Lorraine's stomach tensed. "I've had enough of this
song and dance."

He withdrew a small envelope from his pocket, and Lorraine realized that it held the card from the bouquet. Her
eyes widened and her body began to shudder.

"So you are dating," Paul said. "Wonder what this new
man of yours had to say."

Lorraine lurched forward, trying to snatch the card, but
Paul jerked it out of her grasp. "Give me that!"

"What's the matter?" he asked.

He was creeping her out. "That card is none of your
business. My life is none of your business. We're divorced."

"How long have you been seeing Hunter Holland?"

Lorraine's stomach bottomed out. Oh, God. Paul knew.

"I swear to God, if you don't give me that card and get
out of here immediately, I'm calling the cops."

"And more importantly, why did you think you could
shaft me in the divorce?"

Lorraine lurched for the card again, but again, Paul

ulled it out of her reach. "I didn't shaft you. And my love ife is my business."

"Not if you were cheating on me." The annoying smirk on his face fell flat, replaced by an angry look. "Were you?"

"I'm not even going to dignify that with an answer."

"Fine. But you know what you *do* owe me an answer about? Not disclosing your assets during the divorce. Divorce law in California is very clear. All debts—and *assets*—acquired during a marriage are to be split fifty-fifty."

"Paul, we've been through this." And she didn't care to remember the money she'd lost because he'd invested in a business without her consent that had turned out to be a bogus pyramid scheme. She'd had to share in that debt. "I honestly can't imagine what's gotten into you, but I'm done with this conversation. I'm going to call the cops now."

As she dug her cell phone from her purse, Paul placed the card on the table. Lorraine quickly snatched it up.

"1437 Keele Street," Paul said nonchalantly, as if he'd just announced that there was more sun in the forecast. "Great location, don't you think?"

Lorraine's heart stopped, and an odd sensation spread through her. A numbing sort of feeling that left her light-headed.

"I bet it'll fetch a pretty penny on the market."

Lorraine couldn't speak. Paul was referring to the property Douglas had left her. But how did he know?

Paul took a step toward her, and she inched backward. "Half of that property belongs to me."

"You still have that investigator looking into my life? How dare you!"

"There's nothing you can keep from me. Haven't you learned?"

What was happening? Was Lorraine in the middle of a nightmare? Because this didn't make a lick of sense.

"I—I didn't keep anything from you. I never… I didn't have that property while we were married. Only after our divorce was final."

Paul threw his head back and laughed. "How convenient. You think I'm stupid enough to believe that? You getting that property was in the works *before* our divorce was final. You know it, and I know it."

"You're wrong," Lorraine said, and felt the sting of tears. She didn't understand how this was happening. She balled her hands into fists to avoid actually lashing out at him. And she hoped that by digging her fingernails into her palms and directing the pain there she would stop the tears from filling her eyes. She didn't want Paul to know that he was getting to her.

"You were left in the will *before* that old guy died… while we were still married."

"Get out." Lorraine wanted to slap the smug look off of Paul's face. How had she ever loved him?

"Half of that property is mine," Paul said. "You thought you could pull one over on me, but think again. As a married couple, whatever assets you have, *I* have. Half of that store is mine. And I expect a cash payout."

Then Paul turned and marched toward the door. Lorraine stood, speechless.

Paul opened the door, but then turned back toward her. "You gotta love the state of California."

"Keep dreaming, Paul. You know nothing."

"Oh, really?" His eyebrows shot up. Then he said, in a low, deep voice, "If wanting to spend more time with you is a crime, then I'm guilty."

"What?" Lorraine asked, her eyes narrowing. But Paul just chuckled, then walked out the door.

Lorraine rushed forward and quickly locked the door, then bolted it. Finally, she sucked in a deep breath.

Her body was still trembling, her adrenaline coursing through her at rapid speed. And when she understood Paul's parting words, she doubled over, as though she'd been kicked in the stomach.

Paul had just recited the exact words Hunter had written to her in a text.

No… That made no sense. Hunter must have also written those words in the bouquet's card.

Lorraine quickly opened the card and read.

I know everything. My lawyer will
be in touch soon.

Lorraine's pulse pounded in her ears. What was going on?

She looked at the stunning bouquet, a sinking feeling filling her gut. Hunter hadn't sent the flowers? Paul had sent them to her as a ruse? Some psychotic ploy to build her up, then tear her down?

That's when she crumbled, placing her back on the door and sliding down it until her bottom hit the floor.

She began to cry. Finally, when she was ready to accept Douglas's gift and move forward, Paul had thrown up a roadblock. He was determined to kill her dream just as he had killed their marriage.

Chapter 17

At first, when Hunter saw the text from Lorraine, he thought it was a joke.

Did you send me flowers?

His response had been a smiley face and a LOL, followed by a question mark. Was she playing some kind of joke with him?

"What's so funny?" Omar asked, looking over his shoulder at his phone.

Hunter put the phone into his pocket, then got up from the table and picked up his dinner plate. "Women," he said. "Hell if I'll ever understand them."

"You've already got woman trouble?" Tyler asked. He was seated across the table from him. "You really are filling Omar's shoes, aren't you?"

"You bounced back from that woman who dumped you," Peter said. "Where'd you meet this one? At another bar? And why didn't you call me to hang with you?"

Hunter held up a hand. "You guys are way off base. This is the same woman."

"What?" Peter asked. "How?"

Hunter took a minute to give them the abbreviated version of the story. "Illogically, she knew my old man, so we've had to be in touch."

Peter slapped Hunter's shoulder. "In touch. I'll bet!"

Hunter's phone vibrated in his pocket, and he withdrew it and read the newest text.

Did you? I need you to tell me. Please!

Hunter's lips went flat. "What's wrong?" Tyler asked him.

"I'm not sure," Hunter replied, putting the plate back down on the table. He quickly typed a reply to Lorraine.

No. I never sent you flowers. Is that a not-so-subtle hint? :)

Something told him that Lorraine was upset, but in case she was playing some sort of joke with him, he'd added the smiley face. Though he couldn't understand what kind of joke she could possibly be playing.

Never contact me at this number again.

"What the heck?" Hunter said aloud.

"Hey, man. What's going on?"

Hunter heard the questions from his new friends and colleagues, but he couldn't answer them. Instead, he strode out of the dining hall and into the corridor. He quickly called Lorraine's number and put the phone to his ear.

She answered after the first ring. "I said to never contact me at this number again," she said without preamble.

"Lorraine, what's going on?"

"I can't talk," she said. "I—I think my privacy's been compromised. In fact, I know it has."

"What does that mean?"

"It means I can't talk right now. I've got to go."

"Lorraine? Lorraine?"

But only silence greeted him.

* * *

Once Lorraine had the answer from Hunter, she grabbed the bouquet of flowers, her purse and her car keys and left her townhouse. She marched the flowers to the nearby dumpster and tossed them in there.

On her way to the car, her phone rang again. She glanced quickly at the screen. It was Hunter. She didn't answer.

The last thing she wanted to do was get into an explanation of what was going on over the phone. He would have more questions than she was prepared to answer, and she definitely did not want to provide anything for Paul to monitor. As it was, her anxiety was profound. Just how much had Paul read? Had he been able to access her voice mails? How dare he violate her privacy.

Lorraine got into her car and slumped against the steering wheel. It was hot, the air in the car hard to breathe, but she didn't care. Paul's visit had already left her feeling smothered. He hadn't needed to have an investigator looking into her life. He'd been spying on her via her phone and email accounts.

After several seconds, Lorraine started the car and put the AC on full blast. She was about to text Rosa to tell her that she was heading to her place when she realized she couldn't. Paul knew where Rosa lived. If he was actually monitoring her messages via her Apple ID, then he would easily know where she was going if he wanted to continue to harass her. In fact, what Lorraine needed to do was head to a tech shop and have her phone fixed. Better yet, she could buy another one. Change her number...

No. She wouldn't give Paul the satisfaction. Besides, she would still need to keep her Apple ID or lose all her apps, and other vital information stored in her smartphone and computer. No, she would have the phone fixed—root Paul out of her life, this time hopefully for good.

Lorraine headed straight for Rosa's place, her whole

body taut. She bit down on the inside of her lip the entire drive, until she finally tasted blood. Her level of distress was off the charts. She couldn't believe that Paul had been spying on her, much less that he expected her to hand over half of the store.

And if she had learned anything from the divorce, it was that Paul could be ruthless. He had fought her tooth and nail on absolutely everything, and she believed 100 percent that he would pursue the store. She didn't know if he had a legal leg to stand on, but that wouldn't stop him from making her life miserable.

When her phone rang through the car's Bluetooth system, Lorraine actually flinched. Then she glanced at her dashboard. Hunter was calling.

She quickly pressed the button to reject the call.

Lorraine got to Rosa's place and glanced around to make sure that Paul wasn't lurking anywhere. She wished the horrible thought was simply paranoia, but it wasn't.

"Breathe," she told herself, and forced in several deep breaths. She went to Rosa's door and knocked, but her friend wasn't home.

Back in her car, Lorraine decided to send Rosa the same text she'd sent to Hunter, telling her that she couldn't contact her via her phone until further notice.

The moment after her text went through, another message popped up on her screen. This time from Hunter.

You have me worried. What's going on?

She sat there with her phone in her hand, wondering what to do. Paul's visit had made it clear that he was going to make her life a living hell. He might not be right about his claims, something she could determine with the lawyer. But it was the headache of having to fight with Paul over this. Their back-and-forth fighting during the divorce had been too much emotionally, and she was done. If giving up the store meant peace of mind, so be it. Because on the off chance that Paul was right, there was no way in hell she was going to keep it, sell it and give her ex any portion of it.

But she couldn't explain any of that to Hunter right now. She did, however, have to tell him *something*. So she sent him a brief text.

My phone's been compromised. It's my ex. We can't communicate this way. I'll be in touch. Please don't message me again.

Now Lorraine had to find a tech shop to go to in order to deal with her phone.

Amanda… Didn't she have a cousin who worked with computers? Maybe he could help her with her phone.

Lorraine quickly called her friend. She answered after the second ring. "Hey, stranger."

"You're up, great." Amanda worked the night shift as a personal support worker in a retirement home.

"Yeah. I just got up not too long ago. What's up?"

"I need you," Lorraine said. "I can't explain why on the phone. Can I come over now?"

"Of course."

"All right. See you soon."

An hour later, Lorraine was with Amanda at a small computer shop on the west side of town. Lorraine worried the inside of her lip as she watched Brent, Amanda's cousin, handle her phone.

"This isn't as uncommon as you might think," he said. "Parents typically monitor their children's accounts this way."

Lorraine snorted. "I'm not his child."

"And some exes who don't want to let go continue to monitor an account. Or when they just want to creep a person out."

"I let him set everything up for me because he knew what he was doing," Lorraine said. "I can't believe he would invade my privacy like this."

"I'm not surprised," Amanda quipped. "He probably did it during the divorce, too. Jerk."

Lorraine shuddered at the thought. "Can you fix this for me?" she asked Brent. "Change my passwords, make sure my ex can't access my accounts anymore?"

"I can. I'll need a bit of time."

"You're an absolute lifesaver. Will you have it ready by tomorrow?"

"Sure thing. But when you come back, bring your computer. I'll make sure everything's reset on there."

"Of course. I wasn't even thinking about that." What a pain Paul was being. "Let me just get some of the phone numbers I'll need until tomorrow."

A few minutes later, Lorraine left the store with Amanda. Once outside, Amanda hugged her. "I'm so sorry. You look really stressed."

"I can't believe he's doing this to me." Lorraine had filled her friend in on all that had gone on—including the fact that she'd seen Hunter again. "Why won't Paul just leave me alone?"

Amanda made a face. "You know why he's doing this. Because you left him. He's making you pay for that. That's why he was so evil during the divorce. And now that he learned about the property you were left, he's got another way to stick it to you."

"Paul left our marriage long before I ever made it official."

"You know that, and I know that. But you also know Paul. You think he'll take any responsibility for his own actions?" Amanda gave her a pointed look, as if the answer was clear.

"I knew I should have just signed over the store to Hunter when we were at the lawyer's office a few days ago."

"Why didn't you?" Amanda asked her.

Lorraine didn't answer right away, and Amanda's lips twisted in a scowl. "Come on, don't tell me you've caught feelings for him. He was a booty call. Great in bed, just what you needed. But you're literally just finished dealing with Paul, and if ever there was a sign that you need to concentrate on you and forget about dating, this is it. You can make your dream a reality without accepting handouts."

"I wouldn't call this a handout, Amanda."

"All right, maybe that's not the best way to describe it. My point is, before you ever received the store, you were looking forward to making your dream a reality on your own. If you accept the store, you're going to have to deal with Paul, and you're going to have to deal with Hunter. I just want to see you finally concentrate on you without any distractions. Open your store—on your terms."

On her terms... Amanda's words struck a chord. She was pretty certain that if she accepted Douglas's gift, Hunter would be a part of the deal. He told her that he'd wanted to work with her, and she could see him pursuing that, if for no other reason than to do something in his father's honor. But Amanda made a good point. She didn't have to let him.

"I have a lot to consider. But first, I need to pick up a burner phone. Something to use until I get my phone back tomorrow."

Lorraine stayed in her car for a good few minutes when she got back to her townhouse complex, looking all around to see if Paul was lurking anywhere. Satisfied that he wasn't waiting for her, she got out of her vehicle and went into her unit.

She locked and bolted her door, and only then was she able to relax. She curled up on the sofa and found Hunter's number among the list she'd written down. She started to punch his number into her temporary phone, then stopped.

I just want to see you finally concentrate on you without any distractions. Open your store—on your terms.

Wasn't this the perfect time to *not* contact Hunter? Give herself the time she'd originally asked him to give her? Time to consider on her own, for herself, what she was going to do?

She put the phone down.

Chapter 18

Hunter powered his foot through the last edge of the warped railing, and the wood snapped with a loud crack. He watched the beam fall over the side of the rotting deck. Sweat dripping from his forehead, he looked around with a sense of satisfaction. He was going to fix this deck up, along with the rest of the house. Restore it to its former glory.

Hunter lifted his water bottle from the deck floor and took a long, greedy sip. His cell phone rang—and his hope soared.

The phone was on the concrete edge by the door leading into the house, and he hurried to snatch it up. Was Lorraine finally getting back to him?

Instead, he saw his colleague Peter's photo flashing on the screen, and disappointment washed through him. Not that he wasn't happy to hear from his friend, but he was really hoping to get a call from Lorraine.

Why hadn't she gotten back to him? A few days after the cryptic texts from her, and Hunter was not only confused by her silence, but worried.

He let the call from Peter go to voice mail, because he knew that his new friend was calling about hanging out at a bar tonight. He'd mentioned this morning when they were heading home from their shift. "I'll be your wingman," Peter had said. "I'll happily take the crumbs while you get the cake."

Normally, that might be an offer Hunter would happily

accept. But he didn't feel like it, and he wasn't quite ready to examine why.

Who was he kidding? He knew why. He wanted to hear from Lorraine, but she was shutting him out. Her privacy had been compromised, yes, but why was she still not speaking to him days later?

Unless she didn't like him as much as he liked her.

Hadn't he made it clear to her that he liked her, not just their time in the bedroom? He'd sought her out after the letter from his father because for some reason, he felt comfortable with her. He could be vulnerable with her. Why wasn't she letting him in during whatever issue she was having?

Maybe Hunter had built their relationship up in his mind, and it was nothing more than a fling for her.

Hunter had been alarmed enough to contact the police and ask if there were any reports of problems involving her. There'd been nothing.

Which meant she was avoiding him. Hunter had even contemplated calling her friend Rosa, but refrained. Lorraine had ample opportunity to get in touch with him. If she didn't want to, he wasn't about to hunt her down.

Hunter looked down at the wood beneath his shoes. The beams were warped and cracked. He'd have to replace the entire deck.

He went back into the house and headed toward the fridge for a beer. He had enough to occupy his time without worrying about Lorraine, like getting to work on these renovations.

But the next day, when his colleague Peter told him some crushing news about his cousin, he knew that he had to track Lorraine down.

"Thanks for getting back to me," Lorraine said to Cliff Andrews, the lawyer who'd handled her divorce. "You got my detailed message?" Long-winded had been more like it. She'd blabbed on and on, her anxiety ringing in every word she'd said. But she wanted Cliff to know every detail in order to give her the right answer.

"I did," Cliff said.

"I just want to make it clear that I didn't know anything about the store before the divorce. I had no clue I was being left anything in my patient's will."

"Let me put your mind at ease. It's a nonissue. The date of your separation is the date when your assets stopped being shared, which was a full year before your divorce was final. Douglas Holland became a patient at the hospice seven weeks before his death, so even if Paul wanted to push the issue, he wouldn't have a leg to stand on. We're not talking about one of your relatives where you had a reasonable expectation that you had a substantial gift coming. Besides, the date you were made aware that you'd been left property was *after* your divorce was final. Your ex-husband is not entitled to any of this gift, no matter what he says."

Lorraine sucked in a sharp breath, tentatively hopeful. "You're sure?"

"Absolutely. I've already spoken to his lawyer, and we're both on the same page. He's going to speak to Paul."

"I can't tell you how relieved I am," Lorraine said.

"Of course. Congratulations, by the way. I remember you talking about wanting to open a store. Now you'll be able to."

Lorraine forgot that she'd spoken with her lawyer about this. But it had been at a time when Paul had been drawing out the proceedings, fighting her tooth and nail over everything. Stressed, she'd told Cliff how she couldn't wait for the divorce to be final so that she could concentrate on herself and her dream. Now, it was a relief to know that Paul couldn't sidetrack her plans.

"Thank you," Lorraine said. "You've made my day."

When Lorraine hung up the phone, she was so happy that she wanted to do a victory dance. The next best thing was heading into the pool for a swim.

So she went downstairs to do exactly that. She jumped into the water and began to swim languidly. No need to burn her muscles at full pace as though a demon were chasing her. Today, she could enjoy a brisk yet relaxing swim.

She was on her third lap across the pool and sucking in deep breaths as fatigue was finally getting to her. Once her hands hit the side of the pool wall, she gripped the edge with her fingers and burst through the water. She shook her wet hair, then opened her eyes.

A spasm of terror hit her as surely as if she'd been physically struck.

For a moment she didn't know what to do. Her first instinct was to slip back into the water and swim to the other side of the pool. But Paul would simply follow her, still confront her.

No, there was no point in running.

Paul's lips pulled in a smug smile. "I see you changed your number."

Lorraine didn't bother responding to that. He already thought he was very clever, but at least the problem had been resolved. She'd decided to stick with the new number on the burner cell, in part because she didn't want Paul to have a way to reach her. He wasn't as smart as he thought he was.

"You shouldn't be here," Lorraine said. "This complex is for residents only."

Paul walked toward the edge of the pool. "I don't care what your lawyer says. Half of that property is mine."

So he'd spoken to his lawyer. That's why he was here. "If you spoke to your lawyer, then you know that that's not the case. Even if we weren't divorced already, we were separated. Effectively living separate lives when it came to our marital status. I owe you nothing."

"According to you."

"According to the law. Besides, you and I both know that you're only coming after the store to be a jerk. You get a kick out of making me miserable. Didn't you do enough of that while we were married?"

His eyes widened slightly, as though surprised that she was standing up to him. But hadn't that always been their problem? That she hadn't stood up to him? She'd let him walk over her one time too many. Even during their divorce proceedings. But not this time.

"I'm here as a courtesy to let you know that I'll be seeing another lawyer. Taking this as far as I need to take it. When I finish suing you, you're going to wish that you just agreed to give me what's mine."

Lorraine pushed backward into the water and did the backstroke until she got to the other side of the pool. As she knew, by the time she got there, Paul was already there, waiting for her.

Lorraine climbed out of the pool. Her heart was pounding, but she was determined not to back down to him. He was being a bully, plain and simple.

"What, you think you can run away from this?" Paul asked.

"Fine." Lorraine went to the chair and picked up her towel. "Do what you need to do. Just get lost."

"Hey, Lorraine. Everything okay?"

Both Lorraine and Paul whipped their heads in the direction of the voice. When Lorraine saw Manuel, her shoulders drooped with relief.

"Actually, I'm not okay," Lorraine admitted. "My ex is bothering me."

Manuel took a few steps toward Paul. "Hey, buddy. Beat it."

Paul closed the distance between him and the shorter man, all bravado. "I'd like to see you make me get out of here."

"Oh, Paul. Give it up!" Lorraine told him.

He strode toward her now, and she flinched, but stayed rooted to the spot. He wasn't going to hurt her. At least she didn't believe he was.

He raised a finger and wagged it in front of her face. "This is how you repay me? Seeing someone else and now stealing from me?"

The allegation was so absurd, Lorraine didn't even know how to respond to it.

"Buddy, I'm going to call the police."

"That won't be necessary," came another voice, a booming voice that commanded authority. Lorraine's heart began to pound, but this time from excitement as opposed to fear.

Hunter. She knew it, even before she turned to face him. And when she did, a smile broke out on her face. Her eyes darted toward Paul, and she saw fear flickering in his gaze. Good. Let him deal with a bit of what he was doling out.

Hunter strode toward Paul, his eyes locked on his. He stood over Paul by a good few inches, and his stature and gait showed that he wasn't playing.

"If I ever see you around here again, you're gonna regret that decision. Leave. Now. Or that will be another decision you'll regret. I promise you."

Paul's face twitched, and Lorraine knew he was battling for something to say. Trying to figure out how to come off as tough in the face of a man who was clearly tougher.

"You're not moving," Hunter said.

Paul started to walk. Slowly, but nonetheless he was moving toward the exit gate in the fence around the pool. He quickened his pace, went through the gate, then strode briskly toward the parking lot.

"I'm so sorry about that," Manuel said. "If I'd seen him coming in here, I would have stopped him."

Lorraine waved off his apology. "You have nothing to apologize for. Thank you for showing up when you did." Then she turned to Hunter, smiling tentatively at him. "And you, too. You came at just the right time. Thank you."

"Who is this?" Manuel asked, indicating Hunter with a jerk of his head. "Your new boyfriend?" His eyes danced, saying he approved.

Lorraine chuckled awkwardly, but didn't answer. How could she answer? She didn't know what Hunter was to her, other than a man who'd given her a couple of good times in the bedroom.

"My name is Hunter," he said, extending a hand to Manuel.

"I'm Manuel." Manuel shook his hand. "Nice to meet you."

"Likewise." Then Hunter faced Lorraine. "Can I speak to you for a minute?"

"Of course. We can go to my townhouse."

She felt silly, walking with a towel wrapped around her waist toward her townhouse unit that Hunter had never seen. She'd been avoiding him, and here he had come to her rescue like a knight in shining armor. Same as he had the first night.

They walked without saying a word. When they got into her unit, Lorraine gestured to her left, where the living room was. "Please, have a seat on the sofa. You can turn on the television if you like. I'm just going to go and get changed."

She could barely meet his eyes. She felt bad for not getting back to Hunter before now. Lorraine went into her bedroom and changed into a sundress. She combed her damp hair out quickly and put it into a ponytail. Then she went out into the living room to meet Hunter.

He was standing, not sitting as she expected. He had a look on his face that alarmed her.

Then she realized what the look was. Disappointment.

"That was your ex-husband, I take it?" he asked.

"Yes."

"How long has he been bothering you?"

Lorraine shrugged. "Only recently, really."

"But he's the reason you had to have your phone fixed. He was spying on you?"

Lorraine explained to Hunter what had happened. "He found out about the store because he was accessing my private messages. And he was threatening to take the store from me. But I spoke to my lawyer, and he assured me that the store is mine. I owe none of it to Paul."

"Why didn't you call me about this?" Hunter asked.

"Because Paul is my problem."

Hunter's jaw tensed. "But I could have helped you. Talked to him, done whatever you needed me to do."

"I spoke to my lawyer. Armed myself with the facts."

"And that's what you were doing today?" Hunter asked. "Having a discussion with Paul about those facts?"

Lorraine's back stiffened. Hunter had her on that one. She shook her head. "He said he's rejecting what my lawyer said. He's going to fight me."

"And that's why you could have called me. One thing I hate more than anything is when a guy bullies a woman."

Lorraine appreciated his valor, but she stood by her words. "I appreciate you wanting to help me, but I can take care of myself."

Disappointment flashed across Hunter's face, and for a moment, Lorraine felt bad. She didn't mean to offend him.

"And why didn't I hear from you?"

Why, indeed? "Because… I was stressed out. I just felt I needed time away from…" She made a gesture of a circle with her hand, encompassing the space between her and Hunter. "From us. Especially with the drama going on with my ex."

"And that's why you didn't give me your new number? At least let me know you were okay?"

"I wasn't thinking about checking in with you."

Hunter's eyes widened, and he cocked his head as he regarded her. "I see." But he didn't sound happy.

"I'm sorry," Lorraine said. "I didn't mean to sound offensive. It's just… I've been stressed out. I told you before, I'm barely out of a marriage. My ex is giving me grief. A lot's going on."

"I get it," Hunter said, but Lorraine wasn't sure if he did. Yes, she was fiercely attracted to him, but she wasn't ready for another relationship.

"I have a favor to ask," Hunter began. "Which is why I tracked you down. One of my colleague's cousins just got some bad news. Her diabetes has gotten worse, and she's going to have to start taking insulin injections. He was wondering if you might be able to help her. I told him about you, which is why he came to me with this. Can you talk to her. Give her some advice?"

"Sure. You want me to call her?"

"Actually, Peter was hoping you could go there tonight. If that's convenient for you."

"Oh. Will you be with us?"

"Do you want me there?" Hunter countered.

It felt to Lorraine as if he was asking her something else. Something was off between them, but Lorraine understood what it was. She'd left Hunter hanging, and he wasn't happy about it.

But what were they to each other? Two people who'd had sex a couple of times. Not two people who were trying to build a relationship.

"All right," Lorraine said. "I can make it. What time?"

Chapter 19

Lorraine went out and did some shopping so that she could make some healthy options to bring with her. She made a dairy-free broccoli salad with miso, as well as an apple crumble with coconut oil and no butter. These were tasty dishes with fewer calories, no cholesterol and less fat, which made them healthier. She wanted Peter's cousin to know that as a diabetic, you could still eat tasty food.

At six o'clock, her cell phone rang. She went out to meet Hunter. He was standing outside his car, and her heart thudded when she saw him. Earlier, she'd been shocked and embarrassed when she'd seen him so unexpectedly, which had led to her being a little guarded. Now she was once again seeing him as a man. Tall, dressed in tan pants and sandals with a white T-shirt that hugged his biceps, he caused a flush of heat to spread over her. Why did he always take her breath away?

For a few days, she'd avoided him, hoping that she could gain perspective and put her attraction for him behind her. But the butterflies in her stomach told her that attraction had returned with a vengeance.

His eyes connected with hers and lit up, then widened with surprise when his gaze lowered to the containers of food. He quickly opened the door for her, then walked to meet her. He took the containers from her, and she got into the passenger seat.

"What's all this?" Hunter asked, handing them back to her.

"I figured I'd make a couple of dishes to leave with your friend's cousin. Just a sample of healthier food so she knows she doesn't have to starve or eat only lettuce for optimal nutrition. I made a healthy broccoli salad, and an apple crumble with less fat and less sugar that's still big on taste."

"Ah. That was thoughtful."

Hunter went around to the driver's side and got into the car beside her. A fluttering sensation spread through Lorraine's stomach as he started the car. She felt awkward, and was glad when music filled the car, taking up the quiet space.

"I like you," Hunter suddenly said after five minutes of silence.

Lorraine turned to face him. Her lips parted, but she didn't know what to say.

"It bothers me that you shut me out. After everything that's happened between us, I would think you should know that you could have called me about your ex. To talk, to seek advice…whatever. Promise me you'll tell me if he bothers you again."

Why? Lorraine wanted to ask. Why did he care so much?

"Promise me," Hunter repeated.

"Okay," Lorraine said. "I promise."

Less than ten minutes later, Hunter pulled into the driveway and parked behind Peter's car. By the time he took the key out of the ignition, Lorraine was already getting out. It was as if she couldn't wait to be out of the confined space with him.

The door to Peter's Honda Civic opened, and he appeared. He stepped in front of Lorraine's path and offered her a hand. Then he gestured to the large reusable bag she had.

"I made a couple of dishes for your cousin," Lorraine was saying when Hunter got out of the car. "A sample of the kinds of foods she can eat that still taste great. I imagine she's overwhelmed. I'll explain everything when we're inside."

"I really appreciate you doing this," Peter said. "Hunter's spoken highly of you." He looked in Hunter's direction.

"No problem," Lorraine said. She gave Hunter a quick glance, then turned her gaze back to Peter. "Ready to head inside?"

"Sure thing," Peter said.

She fell into step with Peter, and Hunter walked behind them. His shoulders tensed. He was certain now. Her body language, the distance between them. Lorraine was here, yes, and he was grateful that she'd agreed to help Peter's cousin. But emotionally she was shutting him out.

Twenty minutes into the visit, Peter leaned close to Hunter and whispered, "She seems like a great girl."

"Yeah," Hunter agreed. "She is."

Which made it all the harder to watch her, eyes lit up as she talked to Diane about her qualifications as not only a nurse, but a nutritionist. Hunter could easily picture Lorraine being a part of his life. Problem was, she was pulling away from him.

She was the epitome of loveliness and grace during dinner. Hearing Lorraine's qualifications, Diane willingly opened up about her diabetes predicament. Hunter saw Diane go from stressed and overwhelmed to positive and hopeful.

"You mean I can eat food like this?" she asked after sampling the apple crumble. "This is *delicious*!"

"I used coconut sugar. It's very low on the glycemic index, so much better for diabetics. I also used a bit of coconut oil and no dairy. So yes, you can have this kind of food. Not a ton of it, of course. But it's really important to cut out the fatty fried foods in addition to limiting your sugar. I'll be more than happy to go over a meal plan with you. I have a friend who's a registered dietician—we can both meet with you."

"You're so wonderful to offer me this. Thank you so much."

"No problem," Lorraine said. "Call me anytime."

When Peter, Hunter and Lorraine were heading out the door, Diane gave her a long hug. "Thanks again."

Lorraine's smile was genuine. "You're welcome."

"Thanks so much for meeting my cousin tonight," Peter said when they stepped outside. "You made a strong impact on her."

"I was happy to do it," Lorraine said. Then Peter hugged her.

"And thanks to you, too," Peter said to Hunter.

"No problem, my friend. See you next shift."

Hunter and Lorraine settled into his car. She sighed contentedly.

"You were in your element tonight," Hunter said. "You really gave Diane hope."

"With the help of my dietician friend, we can monitor her blood sugar levels, which I expect to go down rapidly if she follows my suggestions for eating."

Hunter started the car and began to back out of the driveway. "You were great with her. You were born to help people."

Lorraine glanced at him and smiled, and warmth filled Hunter's heart. Again, it was easy to see why his father had taken to her. She was a giving person. Bright, positive. Sweet. And the more time he spent with her, the more he liked her.

But he wasn't going to be a fool and continue pursuing her if that wasn't what she wanted. "Have you given more thought to me working with you?" Hunter asked. "I'm sure you'll need help getting the business set up. I'd love to be a partner."

"You were serious about that?"

"I wouldn't have suggested it if I weren't serious."

"I kind of thought… I figured that was more about your father."

"You mean as a way to honor my father?" Hunter asked. When Lorraine nodded, he asked, "Does it really matter if I want to be involved for that reason? I see the value in what you're doing, and why he wanted to help you do it. When I say I want to be involved, I'm talking for the long haul."

Lorraine glanced out the window and said nothing. Hunter's stomach sank. Why was she so determined to shut him out?

But perhaps more baffling to him was the fact that he wanted to break down her walls. With this many negative cues from any other woman, he'd already have moved on. Yet something was making him hang on here.

He pulled into her townhouse complex in a short while, and that's when Lorraine faced him. "As for your offer, can we talk about it later? I'd just like to think about everything."

"Sure." Pressuring her wouldn't help. If he tried to push the issue, she would probably run.

She offered him a smile. "Thanks again."

Hunter reached behind the passenger seat. He wanted to leave Lorraine with something. Something he'd been compelled to have made for her.

But she opened the door and exited the car.

And she didn't look back.

* * *

Lorraine hurried toward her townhouse unit. Irratio-
nally, her heart was pounding. But she'd needed to get out
of the car and away from Hunter as soon as possible. The
longer she was around him, the more her brain refused
to work properly. All she could think about was the way
he'd held her, kissed her and how she wanted more of that.

Lorraine didn't look back as she went up the stairs to
her door. Didn't look back as she opened the door and
slipped inside.

She locked the door and leaned her body against the
cool metal. Then she blew out a frazzled breath.

There was a knock on the door, and Lorraine jumped,
throwing a hand over her heart. She quickly spun around.
Hunter?

Lorraine stood rooted to the spot. Several seconds later,
there was another knock.

What was she doing? *Just answer the door.*

Lorraine pulled the door open. As she expected, Hunter
was standing there. What she didn't expect was to see him
holding a small gift in his hand.

"You took off so quickly." He extended the medium-
sized yellow box, wrapped in a pale blue bow. "I wanted
to give you this."

"What is it?"

"You have to open it," Hunter said. "That's how you
find out."

She took the box from him. Her heart thudded as she
pulled at the ribbon. Why did she feel so nervous? And
why was he giving her a gift?

"Um, come in," she said, realizing that he was still
standing outside her door.

Hunter stepped inside, and Lorraine wandered into the

living room, where she sat on the sofa. She placed the ribbon onto the coffee table, then pulled the lid off the box.

She glanced at Hunter. The edges of his lips curled in a slight smile, and a flush of heat spread across her chest. "Go on."

Lorraine pulled out the white tissue paper. And when her eyes landed on what lay within, a gasp escaped her lips.

"Oh, my goodness." She lifted out the five-by-seven picture frame and stared at the photo of her and Douglas within it. Douglas was sitting in his wheelchair and smiling from ear-to-ear. Lorraine was standing behind him, her face lowered close to his, a huge smile also on her face.

"Oh, Hunter. This is beautiful." She remembered the day it had been taken. She had been pushing Douglas through the atrium at the hospice, heading for the garden. That's when he'd flagged down a passing nurse and asked her to take a photo of the two of them on his smartphone.

They'd talked a lot about her vision for her store that day, and Douglas had been very encouraging. He'd assured her that as long as she didn't give up, she would make her dreams come true.

"Hunter…" Tears welled in Lorraine's eyes. "This is the perfect gift."

"I found that picture of you two on my father's cell phone. My dad looks frail, but he also looks really happy— as do you. I thought you'd like to have it."

Lorraine held the photo to her chest. "I love it." It brought back the happy moments she'd spent with Douglas. Despite what he'd been going through, he'd remained positive and had given her the kind of encouragement she would have loved her father to give her. "Thank you."

Lorraine rose from the sofa and walked over to the decorative shelf in the center of the living room. She moved aside a glass orb and made room for the photo. The black frame was simple yet elegant. She would cherish it always.

"Maybe you and me meeting the way we did was meant to be," Hunter said, his voice startlingly close. Lorraine turned, surprised to see him right behind her. "My dad clearly adored you. And we connected instantly."

Lorraine's cheeks flushed. She looked up at Hunter, saw that his eyes were molten pools of heat.

"Do you believe that things happen for a reason?"

Glancing down, Lorraine shook her head. "I don't know."

"I think we were meant to work together. I don't care about the financial aspect of the store. I just feel… I feel like I'm supposed to be involved."

"So you believe in fate?" Lorraine asked.

Hunter shrugged. "Maybe I do."

Lorraine's pulse started to race. Right now, she was believing in fate, too. God, help her, every time she was around Hunter, all she could think about was the feel of his hands on her body and that deep sigh that rumbled in his chest when she nibbled on the underside of his jaw.

Just like that, heat pooled between her thighs. She was thinking about sex again. When had she become this woman?

"Um… I…" She glanced away, her voice trailing off. What was she even going to say?

Hunter place a finger beneath her chin and urged her face upward. "What?" he asked.

"I don't know."

"I get it," he said, stroking her face. "I really do. Because I'm feeling the same thing. Confused, yet excited. Something's happening between us. Whenever I'm around you, all I want to do is kiss you, touch you. I can see that you feel the exact same way. And it scares you. It scares me, too, honestly. But I don't think it has to. Maybe we just…go with it."

A shuddery breath escaped Lorraine. But she said nothing.

"We're attracted to each other," Hunter said. "You're divorced, I'm single. There's nothing to keep us apart."

"How effectively can we work together if we're always… drawn to each other like this?" Their physical chemistry would have her wanting to get naked with him all the time.

Hunter's lips spread in a satisfied smile. "Do we really have to think about that right now? Because I can think of a better way to spend our time."

More heat pooled between Lorraine's legs. "That's exactly what I mean."

"Oh, I know."

The man was crazy sexy, and she wanted him with an intensity she'd never experienced before.

Lorraine arched her back, jutting out her chest, and Hunter sank his teeth into his bottom lip. Looping her arms around his neck, Lorraine chuckled. "You want me to kiss you."

"Hell, yeah."

And so she eased up on her toes, tightened her arms around his neck and skimmed her lips across his. "There you go," she said, her voice a mere whisper. "That's a kiss."

"Oh, that's not even close to the kind of kiss I want," he said.

Then he scooped her into his arms, and Lorraine squealed in delight.

"Which way's the bedroom?"

"Up the stairs. Second door on the right."

Hunter smashed his mouth down on hers. Flames erupted inside her, leaving her hot, breathless and desperate with need as his tongue tangled with hers. In a nanosecond, her level of desire exploded off the charts.

Hunter broke the kiss and whispered, "That's better."

"No," Lorraine said. "That's just a start."

"Mmm. I like the way you think."

And then he carried her to the bedroom.

Chapter 20

"Well, *someone* certainly looks happy," Rosa said, leveling her eyes at Lorraine from across the table. "Life seems to be agreeing with you."

Lorraine was out with Rosa, Amanda and Trina at a restaurant, celebrating Trina's birthday.

"It's been a good couple of weeks," Lorraine said, smiling. "No more nonsense with Paul, and I've been working on my plans for the store."

"And having lots of sex," Rosa interjected, raising her eyebrows.

Her friends all laughed, and Lorraine chuckled along with them. "Yes, Hunter and I are enjoying ourselves," Lorraine admitted. She had decided to stop fighting her attraction to him, and go with the flow as Hunter had suggested. It felt good to not label what they were and just enjoy each other.

Amanda sipped some wine, then said, "As long as you remember to keep things in perspective. Did you take my advice? I really think you should reject his offer to work with you."

"I haven't given him an answer yet," Lorraine responded. "However, he reiterated that he's not looking for a financial partnership. Just to be involved."

"Remember Paul," Amanda said. "I'm sure you never saw him as the kind of guy who would go after you financially the way he did."

Lorraine made a face. "Paul was my husband. I'm n
married to Hunter."

"You don't have to be married for someone to go aft
you financially if there's some type of working arrang
ment. All I'm saying is be careful. Have fun if you nee
to, and I agree with Rosa—you certainly seem happy, an
that's great. Just don't get all lost in emotion and start mal
ing bad decisions."

"Girl, why do you have to be such a buzzkill?" Ros
asked, playfully swatting Amanda's arm. "Lorraine i
happy. Look at her. Paul's a different person, and thank
fully he's no longer an issue. Let her enjoy her time wit
Hunter."

"I agree," Trina said. "Don't be so negative, Amanda
I'm not saying she shouldn't be cautious, but let's not thinl
the worst without cause."

Not a moment too soon, a team of servers approached
the table with a slice of cheesecake, in which there was
lit candle. They began to clap, then sang the restaurant'
signature birthday song.

Though Lorraine smiled through the song, Amanda'
words weighed heavily on her. She *was* taking things one
day at a time with Hunter. But the truth was, she really did
like him. Their chemistry was hot, and every time she was
in his arms, he took her to even greater heights of passion
than before. How was that possible?

"You guys!" Trina said, once the servers left the table.
"I told you I didn't want the birthday song."

"On your birthday, you don't get a choice," Rosa said.

"I really wish I could hang out with you longer," Trina
began, pushing her chair back, "but I've got to head to the
theater for that movie with my hubby. I'll see you all later."

They settled the bill, and Trina collected her gift bags.
They exited the restaurant, and all hugged each other before parting ways.

"Don't let Amanda get to you," Rosa whispered in Lorraine's ear. "Keep having fun."

Lorraine forced a smile, but as she made her way to her car, she couldn't stop thinking about Amanda's words. She didn't want to get sucked into a relationship with a man and derail her dreams.

Rosa was the idealist, the romantic. Amanda, the realist. Amanda was right. It was time for Lorraine to concentrate on her goals without any distractions.

So she called the real estate lawyer, and the next day signed the deal to finalize the ownership of the property. Then she spent some time researching contractors after meeting with the lawyer, and made arrangements for one of them to meet her at the store the next day.

It was time she set her plans in motion.

Everything was coming together.

A fire was lit in Lorraine now, in part because of the good news from Diane. No more being afraid, no more holding back. She was focused now, more determined than ever to move ahead with getting her health center up and running. As she watched the contractor take measurements and check the structure of the walls, she couldn't help smiling. Her dream was becoming a reality.

"All right," Clive said, turning to face her. "I've taken all the measurements. Next is getting you an estimate."

Lorraine shook the contractor's hand. "Thank you for coming out, especially on such short notice. Like I said, I'm not 100 percent certain when I'll be moving forward with the renovations. But if you could give me a general idea of the price, that would be great."

Clive nodded. "I'll get you an estimate in the next couple of days."

"Thank you," Lorraine said. The man exited the store, and Lorraine looked around, her lips pulling in a smile.

She could do this. And now that the headache of Paul going after her for a portion of the property was over, she realized how much she wanted this.

She wanted to pinch herself. Why she had connected so strongly with Douglas, she didn't know, but she was beyond elated that he'd chosen to bequeath her this store. He knew how much she wanted to help people, and she couldn't wait to make a difference in a lot of people's lives.

Her phone rang. She quickly got it from her cross-body purse and looked at the screen. Diane was calling.

"Hey, Diane," Lorraine said.

"Hi, Lorraine." Diane's smile was evident through the phone line. "I know you might be busy, but I'm wondering if you're free? I was hoping we could get together. I'd like to buy you lunch for helping me so much."

"Actually, I'm at the store right now. I met with a contractor to see about renovations and another one is due here in fifteen minutes."

"Maybe later, then? I already called Hunter. I figured I'd treat both of you to a meal. If not for him, I wouldn't have met you."

"Oh. Well, how about we plan for later? That works for me, if that's okay."

"All right. I'll call you back. And, Lorraine—thanks so much for changing my life for the better."

Warmth spread across Lorraine's chest. "You getting better is all the thanks I need."

After the second contractor left, Lorraine sat on the sole wooden chair in the room. Unexpectedly, emotion swelled inside her. Her eyes misted and her chest suddenly felt full. Her life was finally falling into place.

Suddenly, a lump lodged in her throat. She swallowed, but she couldn't quite swallow away the bad taste in her mouth.

She should have called Hunter. He'd wanted to be a part of this, and she was shutting him out. He wanted to work with her, and was it really such a bad idea? Surely she would need the help, but she was shutting him out because Amanda had convinced her that she should distance herself from him. But as she sat here in this store, having spoken to two contractors, she found herself wishing she had him here with her to give her his opinion.

Why was she letting Amanda's negative attitude get to her?

She knew why. She had fallen for Hunter, and she was desperately afraid of getting hurt. What if he didn't feel about her the way she felt about him?

When the door chimes sang, Lorraine whirled around in the chair. She expected to see Tom, the contractor who'd just left, reentering the store. Perhaps he'd forgotten to tell her something?

Lorraine's heart spasmed when she saw Paul.

"Hello, Lorraine," he said, leveling her with a grin that didn't meet his eyes. "When are we opening for business?"

A chill swept down Lorraine's spine. What on earth was Paul doing here?

He walked farther into the store, looking around as he did. "This place has potential. I like it."

Though an uneasy feeling was swirling in Lorraine's gut, she got to her feet. She was determined to show Paul that she wasn't afraid of him. "*We* aren't doing anything."

Paul chuckled, an eerie sound if ever there was one. "Oh, I don't think you're getting this. I'm going to have a cease-and-desist ordered on you so fast that you won't be able to open for business. You're going to spend so much time in court that you'll have no money left, and you'll wish you'd just given me half of this business as I asked."

"Asked?" Lorraine chortled. "You didn't *ask* for any-

thing. You've been demanding, thinking you can intim
date me."

"Demanding? Sweetie, you haven't seen demanding
So far, I've been nice."

"I'm not your sweetie. Now get out before I call th
police. You've harassed me enough that I can file a re
straining order."

"This is your last chance to give me what I want."

"You're insane."

"All right, if you want to play this the hard way."

"I'm not going to be bullied by you anymore. I've had
enough—" Lorraine stopped speaking when she saw the
quick movement of his hand. In an instant, she realized
that he was throwing something. The loud cracking sound
caught her off guard, even as her brain registered what it
was. The front window of her store was crashing.

Lorraine screamed. She heard a scream from someone on the street, as well. Two women jumped backward
in fright.

Lorraine's heart was pounding. As her brain processed
what was indeed happening, she saw Paul take off. He
raced through the front door.

Lorraine started after him, hurrying through the door.
"Paul!"

The two stunned women were still standing on the sidewalk. One of them was bleeding. She'd been hit with either
flying glass or the rock Paul had flung.

"Oh, my God," Lorraine said to them, then looked at the
glass that littered the sidewalk. "I'm so sorry. He's crazy."
She watched Paul sprint away. "Call the police."

Chapter 21

Hunter's eyes narrowed as he approached the store. Was that flying glass?

The sound of a woman's scream confirmed that his eyes hadn't betrayed him. Two women jumped backward, just as Hunter saw the man run out of the store.

Paul!

With a sinking feeling in his gut, he watched as Lorraine came rushing out of the store after Paul. He could see the fear and bewilderment on her face. What was going on?

Hunter slowed the car and put the window down. "Lorraine!"

Her shoulders drooped with relief. "Oh, Hunter. Paul's lost his mind."

Paul was running down the street. He got into a car a few spots up.

Hunter put the car into Park and stepped out. He looked at the woman, who had a gash on her head. "Are you okay?"

"I'm okay," the woman said. "Go stop that guy!"

Hunter quickly looked at Lorraine, who seemed unhurt, just frazzled. "I'll help them," she said. "You have to stop Paul!"

It was in Hunter's DNA to render aid, but they were right—Paul had to be stopped.

So Hunter got back into the car and started after Paul, who darted into traffic like a maniac. The driver he'd just cut off blared the horn.

Hunter gave chase, but safely. This was a neighborhoo with lots of foot traffic, and people could step out into th road at any time. When Paul made the first right, Hunte did the same.

As they drove on the next street, there were no cars be tween them, and Hunter sped up. He saw Paul look int the rearview mirror, then shoot a glance over his shoulder He realized Hunter was after him.

Paul made another fast right. Hunter did the same.

As they neared the approaching intersection, Pau quickly got into the left lane. Hunter couldn't move ye because there was a car blocking his path. At the last sec- ond, Paul whizzed his into the left-hand turn lane. But he was looking over his shoulder as he did, and he didn't stop. Hunter saw the impending disaster, and could only watch helplessly as Paul's car plowed into a red Lincoln Navi- gator. Tires squealed, followed by the sound of a boom- ing crash that was almost like an explosion. Somebody screamed.

Hunter glanced into his rearview mirror, saw that no one was immediately behind him, and then he hit the brakes. He quickly pulled his car up to the curb, parked and jumped out. He ran toward Paul's smashed car as a passenger stumbled out of the SUV.

"I don't understand," the older male passenger was say- ing. He wandered to the back of the car. "What happened?"

The front of Paul's car was completely smashed. He ran around to the driver's side. That's when he noticed the first lick of flames coming from the ajar hood.

The engine was on fire.

Paul's head was moving slowly, as if he was dazed and disoriented. Hunter tried the door.

It wouldn't budge.

Damn it, the door was impacted. Hunter needed to get Paul out, or he would burn alive.

Paul's eyes wandered to the left, met Hunter's. In a nanosecond, he seemed to realize the predicament he was in. He tried the door, but it didn't move. That's when his eyes widened, frantic.

"Help me. Help me!"

Help was the last thing Paul deserved. But Hunter was a firefighter, and whether or not Paul was a jerk, he couldn't let him die like this. Not if he could help it.

Hunter tried the back door, found it locked. "Open the locks!" he barked.

Nothing happened. Hunter went back to the front window, but when he looked inside, he saw Paul's eyes rolling backward into his head. Suddenly, he noticed the blood gushing from his forehead. Was he losing consciousness?

"Somebody call 911!" Hunter barked, hoping that someone already had.

He needed something to break the window. If he used his elbow, he'd probably bust it. No, he needed something else.

Of course. There was a tire iron in his car.

The flames were growing, and people were lining sidewalks, frantic. "Do something!" someone cried. "He's gonna die!" another person yelled.

Hunter ran across the street to his car and quickly popped the trunk. He grabbed the tire iron, then darted back to Paul's vehicle. Still no movement from him inside. He was definitely unconscious.

Hunter shielded his face and then busted the back window open. He quickly pulled up the lock, opened the door and slipped into the back seat. Flames were flickering through the dashboard. The heat was already intensifying. This car was going to blow. Hunter knew it.

He didn't have much time. He reached around to the front to undo Paul's seat belt, and thankfully it gave. He heaved, straining, trying to pull Paul's body backward.

The flames suddenly roared, growing bigger, and Hunter knew there was no more time left. With a primal groan, he heaved Paul's body, and felt a jolt of relief when his body began to move. Quickly, Hunter pulled Paul from behind the air bag, until the other man's body slumped against his in the back seat.

The flames grew into a fireball, as if reaching to ensnare the two of them in the back seat. Someone screamed. Hunter tried to back his way out of the car.

And then someone was there, helping him. "I got you," a man said. As Hunter's lower body slipped out of the car, the man wrapped an arm around Hunter and pulled on him, while Hunter yanked on Paul. And then, at last, all three men fell onto the ground. Hunter quickly scrambled to his feet and dragged Paul away. "Get back, everyone!" Hunter yelled, surprised that so many spectators were far too close to the car.

Someone sprinted toward the car with a fire extinguisher. And the next second, the sound of sirens began. Oh, what a wonderful sound that was.

Hunter felt Paul's wrist for a pulse, and finding one, he blew out a relieved breath. The pulse was weak, but it was there. Hunter then searched Paul's body for any visible signs of broken bones or other obvious injuries. He found none other than the gash to his head and an askew elbow, which told him that it was broken.

The fire truck rounded the corner, followed by the ambulance, and people got out of the way. In a flash, firefighters were jumping off the pump truck and quickly running toward the burning vehicle.

"Over here!" Hunter called when the paramedics jumped out of their vehicle, and the man and woman hurried over to Paul.

"My name is Hunter Holland, I'm a firefighter at Station Two. The victim's got a broken elbow, and a laceration to the head. He was conscious when I first got to the scene, but not anymore. His pulse is weak."

The paramedics began to work on Paul. One of the fire-fighters approached Hunter and said, "Great job getting him out of there. You saved his life."

Hunter gave the man a nod, then stepped back into the crowd and watched them all do their jobs. And he felt a sense of pride knowing he was a part of this family of fine Ocean City firefighters. It felt good to be home, back where he belonged.

Hunter's gaze wandered across the street, taking in the sight of the growing crowd. His eyes landed on a familiar face.

Lorraine's.

Lorraine watched the drama unfold with a sense of horrified disbelief. Indeed, she could hardly fathom what was happening. The last several minutes felt like a strange nightmare.

Even from outside her vandalized storefront, where she'd been standing with the two women, she could hear the commotion the block over. The crashing boom, followed by screams. And her stomach had dropped, terror constricting her chest so badly she couldn't draw breath for several seconds.

Hunter!

He must have collided with Paul's car!

There was an alley that led from Keele Street directly through to Twelfth Street. Paul had taken a right at the corner, then had to have taken another right, which had put him almost directly behind her store on the next parallel street over. It couldn't be a coincidence that Hunter had gone after Paul, and now there'd been a crash on Twelfth so loud that she'd been able to hear it.

Lorraine started to sprint, her only thoughts on getting

to Hunter. Tears sprang to her eyes as fear clawed at her chest. *Please, God, let him be all right!*

Paul's crushed car was the first thing she'd seen when she exited the alleyway onto Twelfth Street, and she'd gasped at the sight. Her terror rose. *God, no! Hunter...*

Intense pain gripped her stomach. Lorraine threw her hands over her lips, fear threatening to overwhelm her. Her eyes volleyed back and forth over the horrifying scene. And that's when it clicked that Paul's car was smashed into a *different* vehicle, not Hunter's. An older gentleman was at the back of a damaged red SUV, and he was looking from his vehicle to Paul's. Lorraine could hear frantic cries and jumbled chatter. But where was Hunter?

She saw him at the same time that she noticed the flames underneath the hood of Paul's car! Hunter was at the driver's side of Paul's vehicle, and he seemed to be struggling with the door.

Her heart almost seized in her chest.

She flinched when Hunter smashed the window, and her stomach bottomed out when Hunter went into the back seat of the car.

"No, Hunter," she protested, but her words were a mere whisper.

"Oh, my God, they're both going to die!" someone beside her in the crowd yelled.

The flames roared to life, and a scream erupted in Lorraine's throat. The stranger in the crowd was right. Hunter was going to die. So was Paul.

Lorraine stood, unable to move, her body trembling, as she watched for what seemed like the next few hours. And at last, Hunter emerged from the car with Paul, both of them falling onto the sidewalk. Hunter quickly got to his feet and pulled Paul several feet away.

Was Paul dead? He wasn't moving. Lorraine's heart

pounded furiously. No matter that Paul had been an incredible jerk to her, she didn't want him to die.

The crowd filled in around her, and the action around her was distorted through her tears. Then the emergency responders were arriving. She heard Hunter barking out orders to the crowd. All the while Lorraine could hardly breathe.

And then, suddenly, Hunter was looking at her. She registered the paramedics loading Paul onto a gurney, and felt a rush of relief. He was alive. He had to be.

Amid the chaos surrounding them, the flashing lights of the cop cars, fire trucks and ambulance, Hunter started toward her. He took long, determined strides, and despite the myriad of emotions swirling throughout her, she couldn't help thinking that Hunter looked so heroic. Strong. Fearless. He'd just gone into a burning vehicle to save Paul's life.

Her heart fluttered as he neared her, and then fresh, hot tears spilled onto her cheeks. She pushed through the people surrounding her and rushed toward him. "Oh, Hunter!"

She threw herself at him, and he pulled her into a warm, strong embrace. She cried, relief rushing through her in waves.

"Hunter, are you—"

"I'm fine," he told her.

Lorraine's body shook, and Hunter held her tighter. She never wanted him to let her go.

She finally eased back, but ran her hands down his arms because she didn't want to stop touching him. Her hand ran over the wet, sticky substance on his skin. She quickly looked at him, alarmed. There was a huge gash on his forearm.

"You're bleeding!" she exclaimed.

"I'll be fine."

She touched his face, emotion filling her chest as she did. How close had she come to losing him?

"And Paul...?" she asked.

"He's alive. I couldn't determine any life-threatening external trauma, and the air bag went off, saving him from worse injury. He's unconscious right now, but I think he'll be okay."

Had all of this really just happened? Or was Lorraine in the middle of a nightmare?

Hunter looked down at her. "How long has he been harassing you?"

"He hasn't. I thought he'd finally decided to leave me alone. After you talked to him at the pool, I hadn't heard a peep from him." Lorraine suddenly gasped. "Oh, my God, the women! Paul threw a rock through the window and hit one of them. I was so frantic when I heard the crash, I just ran. I—I had to get to you."

"I'm sure they called for help. But I can make sure an officer goes over there to check on them."

"Hunter, I was so worried!" Lorraine raised her hand to stroke his face again, but he abruptly pulled back, out of her reach.

Her eyes narrowed and her stomach tightened. His lips were taut, his body suddenly rigid. Was he upset with her?

She tried to make eye contact with him, and got her answer when he glanced away. He *was* upset.

"Hunter—"

"You're going to need to speak to the cops. Explain what happened." He paused, his jaw tightening. "You want to have contractors give you estimates, that's your right. The problem is, I keep asking you to include me—not because I want to control you or your decisions. But because I want to be a part of your life. But you keep excluding me, obviously because you don't want the same thing I do. You'd think by now I'd get a clue."

Lorraine's lips parted. Now she understood. He must have spoken to Diane, and he was upset with her for keeping him in the dark about the business.

"I just—" she began, but didn't know what to say.

"Needed time, I know. Funny thing was, I kept expecting that you'd actually call me back. At least give me the courtesy of telling me you wanted nothing to do with me."

Lorraine's eyes bulged. "What? No, Hunter. That's not true."

"Isn't it?" he challenged. "Look, if you felt weird about me helping you with the business, you could have told me that. I'd get it. The point is, just tell me what you really want."

Was that what he was asking her to do right now? Lorraine's lips parted, but she couldn't form any words.

Hunter's jaw tightened. "Look, we need to go talk to a cop." He exhaled loudly. "Explain what happened. Paul's going to need to be charged."

He turned, but Lorraine quickly placed a hand on his arm. The feel of his hard muscles and her body's visceral reaction to him shocked her. Even now, just touching him stoked her attraction for him.

But he wasn't halting, and she had to press her fingers into his arm. "Hunter, wait?"

He faced her. "Wait? For what?"

His question was clear, and yet Lorraine couldn't give him an answer. Even now, she wanted to guard herself from the pain love could cause.

"I'm glad you're okay," Hunter said. "But had you involved me today, even just as a friend, none of this would have happened. Paul wouldn't have gone on the attack if I'd been there."

"He's crazy. He would have lashed out another time."

Hunter didn't look upset anymore, just disappointed— which was worse. "I like you, Lorraine. And when a man likes a woman, he wants to help her. That's all I wanted to do. But you keep shutting me out. You want to know what went through my mind when I saw the window of your store crashing, then saw Paul running away? In that split second before you came out the door..." Hunter's voice trailed off, and his face contorted. "I've never been so scared. I thought you were hurt, or worse."

There was pain in his eyes, and it tore at her heart. He really did care about her. Why was she so afraid of their connection?

"Hey!" Hunter yelled, flagging down the cop who was approaching the crowd. "Officer, we need you for a minute."

The officer smiled at him. "I hear you saved the man's life," the cop said.

"I got him out of the car," Hunter said. "I'm a firefighter with Station Two."

"So that's why you ran into a burning car."

"Occupational hazard," Hunter explained. Then, "The incident started before the crash, however. The man transported to hospital is my friend's ex-husband. He's been harassing her, and only moments earlier vandalized her store. I gave chase when he was trying to escape, and that's when he crashed into the red SUV. My friend and I will both need to speak to officers to give our statements."

Friend. My friend... Lorraine felt sick.

The officer turned to Lorraine. "I can take your statements. Which one of you wants to go first?"

Lorraine looked at Hunter, into his eyes that were filled with hurt. "Hunter," she said, her voice cracking.

"You talk to this officer. We'll talk later."

And when Hunter walked back over to the emergency responders, Lorraine's heart felt as if it were breaking.

Hunter wanted nothing to do with her. And it was all her fault.

Chapter 22

The despair Lorraine felt over the next several days was indescribable. Hunter's words, the disappointment in his eyes, replayed in her mind over and over again. Not until he'd made it clear just how afraid he'd been that she'd been hurt, or worse, had she realized just how deeply he cared for her. Likewise, she'd discovered that day just how much she cared for him.

Those moments as she'd raced down the alleyway, fearing that he had been killed in a car crash, had been the worst moments of her life. And the relief upon learning that he was okay had been profound. All she'd wanted to do was throw her arms around him, hold him forever and tell him that she loved him.

But things didn't play out that way. Fear still had her in its grip. Her relationship with Paul had made her afraid to trust. She kept believing that what she and Hunter had was too good to be true. Doubt had become an anchor, holding her down.

Days after the horrible incident, however, Lorraine had come to realize that she was her own worst enemy. She was letting the actions of another man keep her from a good one. She was finally truly ready to let Hunter in. She had tried to reach out to him, but he'd ignored her.

She kept hoping with each day that passed that Hunter would respond to her, tell her that he was willing to talk, as she'd asked in her calls and texts to him. But a good week after the event, there had been nothing.

When Lorraine's phone rang, she quickly threw off the covers and scooped it up. The hope that Hunter was finally calling was deflated when she saw Rosa's face and number flashing on her screen.

For a moment, Lorraine debated not answering it. She was curled up in bed with a bowl of salt-free kale chips, which she'd dehydrated herself. No more junk food to get her through rough patches.

Nor alcohol. In fact, maybe she ought to go for a swim.

Lorraine pushed the bowl aside and let the call go to voice mail. She settled back on the pillow with a heavy sigh.

Her phone trilled, indicating she had a text. Lorraine looked at the screen, and couldn't help laughing when she read Rosa's words.

If you don't answer the phone when I call again, I'm going to head to your townhouse with the entire Ocean City police department. Don't make me take extreme measures to find out whether you're dead or alive!

And less than thirty seconds later, Rosa called again. Lorraine answered the phone on the first ring. "I'm alive," she said without preamble.

"Well, *thank God.* But in all seriousness, are you okay?"

Lorraine blew out a frazzled breath. "I'm not okay," she admitted.

"I guess you haven't heard from Hunter."

"No. And it's pretty obvious I never will again."

"And what are you gonna do about that? Just accept it?"

"He was all but begging me to tell him that I cared for him at the crash scene, and I couldn't. I have to accept that I blew it and move on."

"Really?" Rosa asked, her tone doubtful. "You're just gonna give up, not even fight?"

"You can't force someone to love you."

"No, but you can push away someone who cares."

"I know I screwed up, but I've tried letting him know that I care. He won't even have a conversation with me."

"You let what Amanda said totally get to you. Suddenly, you went from being happy and hopeful to guarded and glum. I get that you wanted to focus on your business, but you know you figuratively closed the door in Hunter's face. Don't you think he could be feeling insecure, too? Despite what you're saying now?"

"But I've reached out to him. He totally doesn't want to talk."

"So just give up, right? That'll really prove to him that you want to work things out."

"How do I get him to listen to me?" Lorraine asked. "It's not like I'm about to write everything I'm feeling in a text. We need to have a conversation, but if he won't talk to me…?"

"Well, girl, put your thinking cap on. I'm sure you can figure out a way to get his attention. Because unless you want to gain fifty pounds eating potato chips over the next few months, you'd better figure out a way to make him hear you out."

"I'll have you know I'm eating kale chips," Lorraine countered. "Rosa? Rosa?"

But the line was dead.

"Mr. Finkel will see you now."

Hunter rose from the plush chair in the waiting room and followed the secretary down the hallway. He was surprised when she led him into the boardroom, not the lawyer's office.

Joe rose from his seat at the table, extending his hand. "Good to see you again, Hunter. I'm glad you could make it on such short notice."

"You said it was urgent."

Joe nodded. "It is."

The lawyer had briefed him on the phone. Hunter's uncle was disputing the will, fighting over a property that he believed he had rights to, not Hunter.

"All right." Hunter took a seat. "Lay it on me." Perhaps he should have reached out to his uncle, but a lot had happened since he'd gotten back to town. Most notably, he'd been distracted by his relationship with Lorraine. A relationship that had crashed and burned as quickly as it had started.

Hunter swallowed, trying to push thoughts of Lorraine from his mind. Something that had been hard over this past week and a half.

Joe glanced at his watch, then sat at the head of the table. He opened the folder before him. "Ultimately, this might have to go to court, unless you and your uncle can come to some agreement." Joe frowned as he flipped through the pages in the folder. "I'm sorry, I thought I had the original real estate papers in here. I must have left the appropriate file in my office. I'll be right back."

Hunter frowned as the lawyer left the boardroom. Then he closed his eyes and gritted his teeth. This was the last thing he needed. His uncle, Damien, challenging him for property. He didn't have the energy nor the desire to fight it.

When the boardroom door clicked shut, indicating that the lawyer had returned, Hunter said, "Tell my uncle he can have the property. I'm not going to fi—"

The words died on Hunter's lips as he turned. His stomach lurched, and his head swam. What was going on?

The smell was the next thing that hit him, adding to his confusion. His eyes narrowed on the white paper bag in her hand.

"Lorraine..." How was she here? He didn't understand.

"One meathead burger," she announced, extending the paper bag as she approached the table. "I can't believe that's what it's called, but I guess it makes sense. A pound and a half of beef, two types of cheese, bacon *and* onion rings." She shuddered as she placed the large bag on the table in front of him. From within the bag, she pulled out a tall brown paper bag. "Here's your Coors." She placed a second one on the table. "There's also an order of sweet potato fries in the bag."

"What's going on?" Hunter asked.

"I got myself a veggie burger on a whole wheat bun, because I can't really afford the fifteen hundred calories of the meathead burger. I've had too many potato chips this past week already."

"Lorraine—"

"You've been ignoring me," she said bluntly, pulling out the chair at the head of the table and taking a seat. "I'm hoping that over a burger and a beer, we can hash things out."

"But, Joe—" Hunter stopped short when he realized that the lawyer obviously had to have been in on this. "Does that mean that my uncle *isn't* going after the property?"

"I asked him to say whatever he needed to say to get you to come here," Lorraine said. "And I'm not going to apologize. Because I'm not going to put up with you ignoring me anymore."

Her bold statement caused his heart to slam against his rib cage. Conflicting emotions were swirling around inside him. Confusion, shock.

And amidst that, excitement.

Lorraine dipped the bag over and pulled out a burger. She passed it to him. She then took out the other burger, and the order of sweet potato fries in a tin container and clear plastic cover. She lifted the second can of beer and popped it open.

"I'm not normally a beer fan," she said, "but I figured I

can make an exception for today." She nodded toward the food in front of him. "Go ahead. Eat before it gets cold."

Eating was the last thing Hunter wanted to do, but as Lorraine opened the container with her burger and took a bite, he followed suit.

"I'm sorry," she said when she was finished chewing. "I messed up. And for the last week and a half, I've been losing my mind." She sipped her beer. "I guess it wasn't until the day that everything went down with Paul that I realized how much I cared about you."

Hunter felt as though he were in an alternate universe. Lorraine was here, and she'd brought him his favorite burger.

"How did you even know what burger I liked?" he asked, knowing the question sounded ridiculous given everything else Lorraine was saying. But a part of his brain couldn't quite grasp what was happening.

"That day when we went to your father's grave, remember? We were talking about cheat days and what you liked, what I liked."

"Right…" It came back to him in a flash. He and Lorraine on the sofa, watching a movie. Ending the evening furiously making love.

And just like that, heat pooled inside him. Despite everything, he was still fiercely attracted to her. It was the reason he'd had to cut off all communication this past week and a half, because it was killing him to know that she didn't share his feelings.

"And your comfort food is potato chips," Hunter said, remembering. And now her earlier comment made sense. He took another bite of his burger, then washed it down with a swig of beer.

"I think you're forgetting just how recently I was hurt by my ex," Lorraine went on. "I didn't *want* to fall for you. And when I started to care so much, I kept fearing that you'd hurt me, that what was happening between us was too good to be true. Or worse, just a way to pass the time on your part. So I pushed you away. But when I thought you were in a crash with Paul's car, a part of me died. All I wanted to do when I saw that you were okay was hug you and never let you go."

"But you didn't." In fact, Hunter had practically implored her to tell him that she cared about him, and she hadn't.

"Because even then, I was too afraid. I was petrified when I thought I'd lost you, yet it was more terrifying to tell you how I felt."

Hunter swallowed. "When I thought Paul had hurt you, do you know the panic I felt?"

Lorraine nodded. "I do. I saw it in your eyes that day. I didn't know until then how much you cared."

Had he not made his feelings clear? Hunter thought that they'd been on the same page, their mutual affection obvious. "I just wanted you to trust me. With the good in your life, with the bad. To not shut me out."

"I know. But I was too afraid to let myself trust another man." Lorraine's chest rose and fell with a heavy breath. "I heard from Paul, by the way."

"What?" Hunter's heart thudded. "I thought he was remanded without bail?"

"He was. But he sent me a letter via his lawyer. He apologized. Said he realizes how much of a jerk he's been. That he knows he messed up badly and can never make it up to me. He said he also knows that he should have died that day, and he's amazed that you saved his life. According to him, he's a changed man. He's going to plead guilty, take the punishment he deserves and do something positive with his life when he gets out of jail. He went on to say that he's not going to waste the second chance you gave him—and wished us well."

"Really?"

"Yeah. And I believe him." Lorraine put the lid back onto the container with her burger, then rolled her chair closer to Hunter's. "What I'm going to say right now… I know you might hurt me. But I have to say this, and if you reject me, so be it." Inhaling a shaky breath, she placed her hands on his. "I love you. I didn't want to believe I could. I wanted to fight it. But it's true. Our connection, everything between us…it just made sense, no matter what I wanted to tell myself. And without you in my life, I've been lost. I love you, Hunter. But it happened so quickly, and I was afraid of being hurt. That's why I pushed you away. It wasn't you, it was me. I hope you can understand that and give me another chance. Please."

Something finally clicked in Hunter's brain. That this wasn't a joke. That Lorraine was here putting her heart on the line…for him. And suddenly, the walls that Hunter had erected around his heart since the incident with Paul came crumbling down. "You love me?"

Lorraine nodded, her face contorted with emotion. "I do. I didn't want to—I didn't want to love anybody—but I fell for you." She sighed softly. "I don't expect you to feel the same way, but you liked me once. I just want you to let me back in. See where things lead."

Hunter looked into her eyes, saw the vulnerability there. Saw the truth. She was laying her heart bare. "I more than like you, Lorraine. Don't you know I feel the same way you do?" The words fell from his lips, his voice hoarse. "I never expected to fall for you, either. I was afraid, too. How can you meet someone and *know*? Yet that's what I felt. Then you kept shutting me out, and my worst fear was realized. I thought I was out on a limb by myself."

"Oh, Hunter. You're not." Lorraine stroked his face, and the feel of her fingers on his skin sent warmth tingling across his flesh. He turned his face into her palm and kissed it softly.

The feelings of love for her that he'd tried to repress swelled forth, and he pulled her into his arms and onto his lap. Then he slipped his hand into her hair and simply stared into her eyes for several seconds—though what he really wanted to do was kiss her.

Lorraine's eyes glistened as they filled with tears. "Hey," Hunter said. "Don't cry. It's okay. You're here now. We're here. There's nothing to fear anymore. I love you."

Lorraine's eyes widened. "You do?"

"Why do you look surprised?" he asked. "Of course I do. That's why I was so hurt. Look, if you want to do the store alone, I'm okay with that. I don't want it coming between us. I just want to be with you."

"No," Lorraine said. "I want you involved."

"You probably feel funny about it, or uncomfortable and I get that. I'm not upset if you don't want to mix business with pleasure."

Lorraine blew out a shaky breath, and Hunter wiped at a tear that was rolling down her cheek. "There's something I need to tell you. Something else I kept from you."

Hunter's eyebrows shot up, and his pulse quickened. "What?"

"I guess it's better if I show you."

She got up from his lap, and Hunter frowned as he watched her go to her purse. She retrieved her phone, fiddled with it for a moment, then walked back over to him.

"I decided on a name for the store," she said, holding out her phone for him to look at the screen. "What do you think?"

Hunter looked at the photo of a sketch on a piece of paper, clearly some kind of preliminary design. His throat thickened with emotion. "You serious?"

"Do you like it?" Lorraine asked, her voice sounding tentative.

"The Douglas Health & Nutrition Center," Hunter read aloud.

"Something like that," Lorraine said. "As the place fully comes together, we can figure out the name if you're not sold on this one. But I want your father's name to be in there. And I hope you do, too."

"I love it," Hunter said. "My dad would love it, too."

A smile lit up Lorraine's beautiful face. "I'm so glad."

Hunter stood. "Why do you keep doing this to me?"

"Doing what?" she asked, looking at him with alarm.

"Making me crazier about you every time I'm with you," he whispered, then pulled her into his arms. Before she could answer, he brought his mouth down on hers. Intense satisfaction shot through him when Lorraine mewled, and her body relaxed against his.

Oh, how he loved this woman.

Lorraine snaked her arms around his neck and surrendered to the kiss, opening her mouth wide, trilling her tongue with his. Hunter tightened his arms around her waist, heat roaring through him.

But more than anything, he felt happiness. And love.

Easing back, he said, "I love you. And you honoring my father in that way…it means the world to me."

Lorraine smiled at him. "He was such a special man," she said softly. "I loved your father. He was so wonderful to me, and I honestly saw him as a father figure. Never in my wildest dreams did I expect to meet his son and fall for him. That was the greatest gift I could have received, not the store."

"Maybe it was meant to be," Hunter said, then kissed her lips softly. "Because everything about you and me… it's right. I feel it."

"I feel it, too."

Hunter smiled down at Lorraine and framed her face. Then he kissed her again, his mouth lingering on hers. She strummed her fingertips across the back of his neck. Desire coursed through his veins, and with a groan, he pulled back.

"We've got to stop this…or Joe might come back in here and…well, it'd be pretty embarrassing for all of us."

Lorraine chuckled. "I know, baby. I can't even think rationally when I'm around you."

"I love you," he said again, his heart feeling full for the first time in years. It felt good to tell her this. He wanted to tell her how much he loved her for the rest of his life.

"Oh, baby. I love you, too."

Lorraine pulled her bottom lip between her teeth, and heat zapped Hunter's groin. "Don't do that," he said huskily. "You know I'm powerless to resist you when you all but beg me to kiss you."

"I can't help it."

Hunter gave her lips a quick peck, then took her hand. "How about we get out of here?"

Lorraine winked. "I thought you'd never ask."

* * * * *

KIMANI™
ROMANCE

COMING NEXT MONTH
Available October 17, 2017

#545 TAMING HER BILLIONAIRE
Knights of Los Angeles • by Yahrah St. John
Maximus Knight is used to getting what he wants, so seducing gallery owner Tahlia Armstrong into turning over her shares of his family's company should be easy. But when a shocking power play threatens their passionate bond, Tahlia must decide if she can trust Max with her heart.

#546 A TOUCH OF LOVE
The Grays of Los Angeles • by Sheryl Lister
After an explosion shattered Khalil Gray's world, café owner Lexia Daniels becomes the only person he can't push away. The ex-model is happy to explore their chemistry as long as it means resisting real emotion. But playing by his old rules could cost him the love he never thought he'd find…

#547 DECADENT DESIRE
The Drakes of California • by Zuri Day
Life's perfect—except for the miles that separate psychologist Julian Drake from his longtime love, Nicki Long. So when the Broadway dancer returns to their idyllic town, Julian is beyond thrilled. But Nicki's up against a deadly adversary that could end her future with the Drake of her dreams…

#548 A TIARA UNDER THE TREE
Once Upon a Tiara • by Carolyn Hector
Former beauty queen Waverly Leverve can barely show her face in public after an embarrassing meme goes viral. But business mogul Dominic Crowne wants to sponsor Waverly in a pageant scheduled for Christmas Eve. Can he help her achieve professional redemption and find his Princess Charming under the mistletoe?

Get 2 Free Books,
Plus 2 Free Gifts—
just for trying the
Reader Service!

LOVE
Harlequin
romance?

Join our Harlequin community to share your thoughts and connect with other romance readers!

Be the first to find out about promotions, news, and exclusive content!

Sign up for the Harlequin e-newsletter and download a free book from any series at **www.TryHarlequin.com**

CONNECT WITH US AT:

Harlequin.com/Community

 Facebook.com/HarlequinBooks

Twitter.com/HarlequinBooks

Instagram.com/HarlequinBooks

Pinterest.com/HarlequinBooks

ReaderService.com

 HARLEQUIN®

**ROMANCE WHEN
YOU NEED IT**

HSOCIAL2017

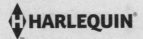